REINA FOX

Savage Tethers

Contents

1

Savage Tethers

2

Chapter 1

Sariah slipped through the veins of the Maw like a starved predator, unseen but always hunting. Her bare feet were soundless as she prowled the damp, filth-strewn cobblestones, moving with purpose, always watching. In the shadows, survival was the only law that mattered, and Sariah knew every twist of that code by heart. The stench of piss, rotting fish, and bodies packed too tight clung to the narrow alleyways, a noxious perfume of desperation saturating the air. But she barely noticed. To her, it was the scent of home, the odor of a place that had never cared if she lived or died, and where she thrived because of it.

Duskhaven's streets were a predator's playground, and she was as good as any hunter who prowled them. She kept her focus sharp, her eyes on the prize, always thinking of the next score, the next scraped-up meal to keep her strong enough to fight another day. There was no room for weakness, no space for distraction; not when the city itself would chew you up and spit you out for the crows. She never stayed too long in the same spot, never let herself be caught in the open.

The brutal law of Duskhaven was simple: see a chance, take it before someone else did. Like the half-conscious drunkard stumbling from a shuttered tavern, his coin purse dangling loose at his side.

Too easy.

Sariah's fingers slipped in, stole what she needed, and vanished before his next breath, leaving him to stagger off without a clue. A few coins, a rusted key, and a scrap of paper with scribbled nonsense. Nothing particularly useful. The man was pauper-broke. Still, she knew how to make even the smallest gains stretch. It was enough to get by. For now.

Sariah didn't waste a second lingering. She pressed on with relentless speed, weaving between tattered laundry lines and sagging market stalls, her instincts sharp, her eyes scanning for the next opportunity. A child ran past her, filthy and barefoot, clutching a loaf of bread like it was made of gold. She glanced at the boy, her childhood mirrored in his escape. Let him have it. She had bigger scores in mind.

At the alley's end, she reached her mark; a crumbling tenement building, hunched and mean, waiting for her like a wounded animal. The bricks were cracked, and the fire escape rusted to hell, but it was home turf, territory she knew by scent and sight. She surveyed it with a predator's eye, sizing up the quickest route, her next move already in her mind.

She climbed with a precision that spoke of practice, her body a map of old scars and lessons learned the hard way. Her claws scraped metal, and her legs burned with the effort, muscles furious but never flagging. The old structure groaned under her weight as if it might collapse and swallow her whole, but she trusted her instincts. It held — barely.

With a deft leap, she caught the ledge, hauling herself up in one smooth motion. Her claws scraped against stone, her muscles burning as she climbed higher.

By the time she reached the rooftop, her breath was steady, controlled. A lifted lock on a back door. A discarded purse at her feet. Another night survived.

Then the scent hit her; copper and sweat, thick with violence.

She turned, crouching at the rooftop's edge, her sharp eyes burning like embers as they narrowed in on the scene unfolding below. It was chaos. A warning. A savage grin flickered across her lips, there and gone. Overconfident and vicious, the wolves moved like a storm through the street, tearing their prey apart with vicious and brutal precision. They left nothing standing in their path, and their target was obvious — the lioness had seen them hunt before. This was Kane's pack, and the gang too slow to scatter never stood a chance.

One wolf lunged, its jaws clamping through fabric and flesh, ripping through the air with a sound that sent a shiver of anticipation down Sariah's spine. The scent of blood hit her first, sharp, metallic, intoxicating. Then came the spray, misting the air like fine red mist. Another wolf leapt from the shadows, sending a rival gang member crashing into a graffiti-stained wall, the wet crunch of bone breaking under impact echoing even above the noise. Sariah watched, the violence as mesmerizing as it was terrifying. The wolves' prey never had a chance. They carved through them like the city itself, leaving the survivors to crawl away, bleeding. The battered gang would be lucky to see the next sunset.

The street was a riot of color and noise, alive with the copper tang of fresh blood and the screams of the fallen. Shattered glass caught the dim light, reflecting the chaos in jagged fragments. It was a sight she knew too well; the wolves taking what they wanted, as they always did. Quick, cruel, and unstoppable. She bared her teeth at the display, feeling the old emotion twist inside her, sharp as a blade and just as cutting. Envy.

Sariah stayed still, barely breathing, watching as the pack dismantled the gang with practiced efficiency. This was Duskhaven at its purest, power feeding on weakness.

This city didn't belong to her kind. She had no pride. No allies. Just herself. And that was the way it had always been.

By the time the last body hit the ground, she was already moving.

The tenement roof was a sanctuary of speed, and Sariah didn't slow her pace. She was a ghost over the city, a streak of shadow and claw, leaping rooftops with feral precision. Each bound was a heartbeat, each landing a promise. She was untouchable, a ghost in the cityscape. The wind tore past her ears, and though her limbs ached from exertion, she pushed harder. She was testing the limits of her strength, feeling the pulse of the hunt in her muscles. In Duskhaven, recklessness was a death wish, but she thrived on the adrenaline, letting it sharpen her senses. She couldn't stop until she was certain, until she knew her turf hadn't changed.

Slipping through back alleys, descending like a thief on the crumbling fire escapes, she found her way to the abandoned loft, hidden behind a boarded-up storefront. She dropped down the final ledge, landing in a crouch, her ears straining for any hint of trouble. Had the pack tracked her here? She scented the air, tasting the dust and the damp stone. Nothing. No wolves. Still her territory. She eased through the splintered doorframe, eyes and ears alert, unwilling to let her guard down.

Inside, the thin slice of comfort she called home felt both familiar and fragile. The air was stale with dust and disuse, and the floorboards creaked under her careful steps. She scanned the space for anything out of place, any sign she wasn't alone. Nothing. The silence was as thick as the gloom, and she felt it wrap around her like an embrace. Unsettling, but hers. The way she liked it. Safe enough to risk a night's rest — safe enough to believe she was forgotten.

With a quiet exhale, Sariah shut the heavy metal door behind her, securing the deadbolt before setting her dagger on the splintered table. The distant echoes of the city's violence hummed beneath the silence of the loft.

She leaned against the cracked wall, the weight of another night's survival pressing down on her like the city itself. She listened, still expecting the wolves' approach, imagining the sound of claws on stone and breath like thunder. It wouldn't have been the first time Kane's pack had tracked her down. But there was only her heart's frenetic beat. She let herself relax a fraction, feel the old familiar solitude and the absence of everything but herself. Was that freedom? Or just another breath stolen from the jaws of the Maw? She could never tell the difference.

The evening echoed fresh in her mind, repeating like a cruel joke. The chaos. The violence. The wolves' attack was a warning, brutal and unmistakable. No one was safe in this city. Especially not on the rooftops, where one good fall would end a life faster than any blade. The pack had torn through their rivals like beasts possessed, and she had watched from above, just out of reach, longing to be untouchable and fearing she never would be. This city wasn't hers. This territory wasn't hers. She had no pack. No family.

That was the way it had always been.

But Sariah was a survivor. If the Maw taught her anything, it was that the quickest cat got the kill. She wasn't afraid to run, wasn't afraid to leap. Better to keep moving than to be pinned down and gutted. Better to be alone than dead in a back alley.

She closed her eyes for a moment, hating that she admired Kane's pack as much as she despised them. Maybe more. Strength was the only law here, and the wolves were kings. She was just another hunter in a city full of them, swift and ruthless but never quite enough. Never quite there.

She opened her eyes, adjusting to the dimness like a predator coming awake.
   Another night.
   Another stolen breath of freedom. But in Duskhaven, nothing stolen was ever free.

3

Chapter 2

The Howl was stifling, thick with heat, sweat, and the metallic stink of blood. A cage full of wolves, and Kane was the only one holding the key. It writhed in heavy waves, mingling with the ripe stink of sweat and ungoverned testosterone. Kane held his ground in the center of the room, the steel core to spiraling chaos, as his pack encircled him, their impatience a nearly tangible presence. The scent of raw alcohol and coppery blood crawled over the exposed concrete, lingering in the air like an open wound. Every breath was an effort, every heartbeat a struggle against the claustrophobic space.

The dim light overhead shuddered and sputtered, casting jagged, shifting shadows that danced with the threat of violence, each shadow a mirror to the jagged tension. The light traced the sharpness of jawlines clenched in anticipation and the bulging fists of men bred for war. Battered crates masqueraded as tables, old bloodstains dull against the wood, whispering tales of past conquests and the hunger for more. Kane stood beneath the flickering glow, his face half in darkness, half illuminated, the duality echoing his dominance and the simmering rebellion.

His Beta, Luka, kept close watch, a forceful presence at Kane's shoulder, arms crossed like barricades of muscle. His eyes swept the room, a silent warning that was clear to every wolf present: defy the Alpha and pay in blood. It was a warning Kane didn't need but welcomed nonetheless. The restlessness was a hunger gnawing at their guts, yearning for the next battle to sink their teeth into. Not enough blood, not enough war. They had tasted too many easy victories, leaving their thirst for violence unsated and the pack on edge, eager for the next fight to call their own.

Every squared shoulder and defiant gaze begged for action, for orders that would let them tear through the city like a force of nature. They craved a target, a promise of dominance, a war to set them free. But for now, Kane let the tension build, taut and ready to snap.

He let the silence stretch, let them feel it.

Then, finally, he spoke.

"We take The Veil tonight. If you have a problem with that—" Kane's eyes drag over the room, slow and unforgiving "—then get the fuck out now."

His voice was low, even, but it rolled through the room like a growl of distant thunder.

"We take it. We hold it. We make them remember who owns this city."

His words should have been final, an iron law laid down for all to follow. Instead, the pack shifted around him, their unease nearly thick enough to taste. It crackled in the air, charged and dangerous. Kane felt it rising, a wave of unrest swelling in defiance. He could see the seeds of doubt scattering among them, challenging his command, questioning his strategy. Dissatisfaction spread like a contagion, infecting each wolf with a craving for more immediate, explosive action. Before his words even finished settling over them, someone in the back scoffed, a sharp sound like a blade drawn in threat. Kane's gaze snapped to the source with lethal precision.

Marko.

Big, broad, and dumb enough to think he had something to prove, he stood at the edge of the room, a smirk pulling at his lips. The tension from the pack fed him, emboldening him. He didn't step forward—not yet—but rolled his shoulders, cracking his neck like he was testing Kane's patience. Egging him on. Kane's ash-gray eyes glowed with the heat of a rising storm as Marko challenged him with a voice both casual and sharp at the edges.

"How many bodies are you planning to burn this time, Alpha?"

A murmur of agreement rippled through the pack, a dangerous wave feeding off Marko's audacity. Kane let it roll, unchallenged, for half a second. Just long enough for them to taste what it felt like to have a voice. Long enough to let them believe they had any say at all. Then he spoke again, cutting through the dissent like a blade.

"We're wolves." His voice was quieter this time, deadlier, coiled with menace that dripped like venom. "Since when do we count bodies before a fight?"

He looked at Marko, daring him to push further.

Marko smirked like he had expected that answer, a cocky grin that said the Alpha wasn't as untouchable as he thought. A grin that admitted nothing, not even fear.

"Since we started losing them."
That did it.
The murmur turned into something heavier, something close to a growl, and Kane's grip tightened into a fist.
Another voice.
"What about The Hollow?"
This time it was Garrick. The bastard always had a trick up his sleeve. Lean and fast, he had the shifty eyes of a gambler and the slick smile of a snake. He liked playing both sides, pretending to run with the pack but always keeping one foot out the door. He didn't bother to hide the challenge in his voice as

he called out to Kane, gesturing toward the faded map pinned haphazardly to the wall. "The Veil's locked up tight," he said, his calloused fingers dragging over another district. "The Hollow's weaker. Less of a fight." He talked like he already had it all figured out, like Kane's plan was a waste of time.

A few grunts of agreement rose from the crowd, each one fueling the fire of rebellion. The pack shifted, and Kane's jaw ticked. Luka was already tensing beside him, ready to put Garrick down, ready to turn the insubordination into a bloodbath. But Kane lifted a hand, ordering restraint, his cold eyes never leaving Garrick's face. He wanted them to see this, to feel the weight of his command pressing down on them.

"You want easy?" he asked, his voice silk-soft but full of venom.

Garrick hesitated, his game thrown. He wasn't used to being called out so directly, being the one on the defensive. The silence stretched, long enough to fray the nerve of even the most seasoned fighter.

And Kane smiled. It was the smile of a predator, of a wolf who knew the kill was already his. "Then go be a dog somewhere else."

The words landed like a punch. Garrick's hand twitched toward his knife, the instinct of a coward looking for an out.

Luka's breath stilled, his muscles coiling like springs, waiting for Kane to give the order, to unleash hell. The room balanced on a knife's edge, the tension a razor that threatened to spill blood at any moment. All eyes were on them, watching, waiting, the air electric with the anticipation of violence.

Garrick's face twisted, as though torn between ego and survival. It appears he wanted this fight, probably craved it. Kane was an Alpha, and every instinct should have screamed at him to back down, to know his place and submit or die. His hand shook, hovered near the blade, as though unsure whether to fight or flee.

He didn't get the chance to decide.

"How many bodies are you planning to burn this time, Alpha?"

Kane struck. Fast. Sudden. Garrick flinched, instincts converging in panic, but he didn't get the chance to reach for his blade. The closed in, the shadows collapsing, warping, until Kane was in front of him, gripping his throat, shoving him back against the wall with force. The crates rattled. A glass bottle tumbled off the table and shattered. Garrick's head hit the wall with a sickening thud.

"Touch that knife again, and I'll feed it to you through your fucking throat." His words were ice, freezing Garrick's defiance in an instant.

Garrick choked, his pulse hammering against Kane's fingers, his eyes wide with a fear he couldn't hide. The stillness spread like a plague, infecting the rest of the pack, leaving them barely breathing, frozen as Kane's grip squeezed the fight out of the man who had dared to stand up.

"You don't like my orders?" Kane's voice dropped to a whisper, softer than a blade sliding through flesh. "Then try me."

Garrick's pulse hammered harder as he stared into the lethal cold of Kane's eyes. He didn't try. He couldn't. Even as his fingers twitched toward his knife, Kane's power was a noose around his throat, tightening until the world spun, until every instinct screamed at him to stand down, to beg for air, to submit. Kane held him there for a moment, a second that felt like an eternity, just long enough for the message to sink in, for Garrick to know how close he was to dying. Then he dropped him, letting the weight of his authority hit the pack harder than aftershock.

Garrick staggered, gasping, but Kane didn't spare him another glance or the satisfaction of acknowledgment. He turned, his gaze sweeping over the rest of them, daring them to say another fucking word, challenging each wolf to betray the scent of fear that now clung to the air. No one did. Not even Marko, who had thought he could ride on Garrick's boldness.

The silence roared around them, charged with adrenaline, with the vivid memory of Kane closing the gap in a heartbeat, of the Alpha who didn't need a pack to take what he wanted. It was a reminder of why he led them, why they followed.

Kane's lethal calm cut through their unrest, set it bleeding on the floor. He had baited the challenge out of them, put it to death before their eyes.

"We move on The Veil tonight," Kane repeated. Final. Absolute.

Luka nodded.

The rest of the pack stayed silent.

But Kane saw it.

The glances exchanged, the way Marko clenched his jaw like he was biting back something he'd regret.

This wasn't over.

They'd follow him — for now.

But the moment Kane showed weakness?

They'd tear him apart.

The silence wasn't submission. It was a calculation. Waiting. Planning.

Kane turned, walking out of The Howl without looking back.

He didn't have to.

If anyone tried something tonight, he'd smell the blood before it hit the floor.

4

Chapter 3

The mansion in Serpent's Row seemed like a job too easy to ignore. An enticing mark in a city that offered few. Those baubles were going to buy her a lot more than food this time. Sariah had watched the merchant for weeks, learned his movements, his habits, and grew certain she was dealing with just another rich fool who believed armed guards and high walls made him untouchable. She'd mapped their shifts, following them with the patience of a predator until she could predict every step.

That night, she'd slipped in under a moonless sky, her footfalls softer than the shadows cast by the flickering streetlamps. Now, she moved like a whisper over the hardwood floors, sharp golden eyes scanning the dimly lit study. The space reeked of opulence, with paintings in heavy frames lining the walls, a crystal decanter of amber liquid glinting in the low light. Sariah ran her fingers along the edges of a mahogany desk, smirking as she found what she was looking for. The old oak safe sat nestled behind it, its iron surface worn from years of use but sturdy enough to guard whatever treasure lay inside. It was almost too perfect.

She slid a set of lockpicks from the pocket of her leather vest, crouching before the safe like it was an altar meant for her alone. Her fingers danced over the

13

tumblers with deft precision, metal softly clicking as she coaxed the lock open. This was what she was made for. The thrill of it rushed through her veins, and she could almost taste the payday ahead. She was good, too good, and part of her knew it. This was going to be easy, in and out before anyone knew she was ever there. The air felt too thick, pressing against her skin like a warning. Sariah had been in bad situations before, but this was different. This was wrong.

She felt it before she saw him; the weight of a predator pressing against her instincts, the hairs at the nape of her neck rising as if the city itself were warning her.

Her fingers were light on the lock, her body tense but practiced. The safe in front of her was sturdy, old, but nothing she couldn't handle. A few more twists of the pick, a little pressure and then the scent hit her.

Deep. Dark. Musky with the sharp bite of something raw and uncontained. A scent that wasn't supposed to be here. A scent that reached into her gut and yanked.

Her breath stilled.

She turned slowly, every instinct screaming at her to run, hide, fight, anything but what she was doing now.

Kane stood in the doorway, watching her.

Not moving. Not speaking. Just watching.

The dim light carved shadows across his sharp jawline, his broad shoulders blocking the only exit. The wolves earlier had been vicious, rabid. Kane was something else. Stillness wrapped around him like a noose, his presence a silent promise of violence. His ash-gray eyes tracked her like a hunter contemplating whether to kill or play with his food.

Sariah forced herself to breathe. Forced her voice steady. "Didn't realize you left the door open for guests."

He didn't answer.

He took a step forward instead. Slow. Measured. Like he had all the time in the world to close the space between them.

She shifted her stance, subtly, adjusting her weight for a fast retreat. But Kane saw it. His gaze flicked to her feet, then back to her face. The corner of his mouth tilted—not a smile, something darker.

"Run," he murmured. "See what happens."

Sariah knew a bluff when she heard one.

This wasn't a bluff.

Her pulse hammered against her ribs. She weighed her options: A full-speed sprint to the window? Too risky. He was too fast. A blade to his ribs? Even riskier—he looked like he'd enjoy it.

He moved again, casual, slow, but closer.

Her lungs tightened. "Do we have a problem?"

Kane tilted his head slightly, considering it. "Not yet."

Another step.

Her back hit the desk. Trapped.

His eyes flickered down to the safe, the tools, the evidence of exactly why she was here. His smirk deepened. "So, little lion," he murmured. "What exactly were you hoping to steal?"

Sariah bared her teeth in something close to a smile. "You wouldn't believe me if I told you."

"Try me."

His hand lifted slowly, as if testing to see if she'd flinch. She didn't. She wouldn't. But the moment his fingers brushed a loose strand of hair from her face, she felt it.

Heat. Electricity. A static hum in the air that set every nerve in her body on fire.

No.

Not this. Not with him.

Kane inhaled sharply. His pupils dilated, something feral flashing behind his eyes, and Sariah's stomach dropped.

He had scented her.

A low growl rumbled from his throat, not angry—not quite—but hungry. Like he had just discovered something he had no intention of letting go.

Her breath hitched. Her muscles coiled tight.

"Run," Kane whispered again, this time softer, almost amused. Daring her.

Sariah ran.

She twisted, shoving her weight against the desk for momentum, a blur of movement as she bolted for the window. But she barely made it a step before Kane moved — too fast, inhumanly fast — and suddenly she was spinning, her back slamming against the stone wall, his hand braced beside her head.

His other hand closed around her wrist, tight, firm, but not crushing. Not yet.

"Too slow," he said, voice like smoke and ruin.

Her breath came fast, sharp. Her heart pounded so loud she was sure he could hear it. His grip was like iron, his scent everywhere, drowning her senses. She should have been afraid. Maybe she was afraid. But worse than that, her body liked the danger.

She curled her lip in a smirk, forcing herself to meet his gaze. "Maybe you're just too fast."

Kane leaned in slightly, enough for the heat between them to turn suffocating. "Maybe you're just mine."

Her stomach clenched. No. No, no, no.

Sariah wrenched her arm, twisting with everything she had, and —

She escaped.

Not because she had outmaneuvered him.

Because he let her go.

And that was worse.

5

Chapter 4

Running for her life in Duskhaven felt like drowning in an alleyway of knives.

Sariah's lungs felt raw, her legs screamed with every stride, but she couldn't stop. Not with the howls snapping at her heels. She sprinted through The Veil, the district wrapping around her like a tangle of secrets and shadows. Its narrow alleys coiled between looming structures, paths twisting like lies; a perfect place to lose anyone reckless enough to come after her.

If that someone wasn't the Alpha.

She cleared a barrier of broken crates with the speed of a hunted animal, her feet striking the cracked stone as she landed. She didn't have to look back. She felt them coming, the pack's presence sinking into the city like blood into stone. That bastard had her scent now, and he wouldn't stop until she was back under his control. She pushed harder, knowing she had to disappear, had to dig herself so deep into this den of thieves that even a relentless alpha would think twice before following.

Or she'd need a damn good ally.

He was probably enjoying this. Her entire world was thrown into chaos, and he was chasing her like she was some prey to be broken. But she was a lioness; she'd show him who was broken by the end. Sariah veered into an even narrower passage, hoping her knowledge of this district would keep her a step ahead. The streets twisted in her path, forcing quick changes, faster decisions.

Then she heard it—the howl, echoing and hungry. Too close.

Her heart pounded faster than her racing feet. She vaulted a crumbling wall, muscles and bones protesting, and kept moving. Every breath was fire, every turn a gamble. How many wolves had he brought? Even one was too many with Kane leading the hunt. His kind didn't give up. Not until blood was spilled. Sariah ducked under a low-hanging sign, slipped through a crack between two imposing buildings, and let instinct guide her deeper into the maze. Didn't matter where, so long as it wasn't here. She needed to outsmart him, needed...

She crashed into something solid. Someone. But instead of stumbling, of reeling back, he caught her like he'd been expecting her to run straight into his arms.

"Well, well. If I'd known you'd come crashing into me like this, I'd have prepared a proper welcome." A smooth voice murmured, arms catching her before she could stumble. "Not often I get tackled in the middle of the night. Should I be flattered?"

Sariah jerked back, claws flexing, but the man in front of her only grinned. He was lean where Kane was all brutal muscle, sharp-eyed, and relaxed in a way that screamed danger without even trying. Dark hair fell messily over his forehead, and there was something almost too charming about the way he tilted his head, studying her.

Ronan.

She didn't know much about him, other than the fact he was a raven shifter with a well-earned reputation for making problems disappear faster than she could blink. One of the wildcards in Duskhaven's deck, always ready to make his move when it might stir the most chaos. How much could she trust a trickster like him?

"Not in the mood," she snapped, stepping back.

"Get the fuck out of my way."

"Now, now." Ronan's grin widened. "Where's the fun in that?"

Instead of obeying as a smarter man might, Ronan slipped smoothly into her path, mischief and a hint of something darker playing in his eyes. A flicker of amusement crossed his face, and his grin widened.

"You've got Kane's scent all over you, little lion," he said, mocking and curious all at once. "And from the way you're running, I'd say things didn't end on the best of terms." Sariah clenched her jaw. Who else had picked up the Alpha's trail on her? And what was Ronan's game here, throwing himself into the middle of it?

Of course he could smell it. Shifters always could.

"Not your business."

"Maybe not." He gave a carefree shrug that only pissed her off more. "But if you need a place to lie low, I happen to have one."

She narrowed her eyes, every instinct screaming not to trust this. The last thing she needed was to walk blindly into an alliance she didn't understand. "And why the hell would you offer me that?"

Ronan smiled, slow and sharp. It was the kind of smile that promised both protection and betrayal, and it set her nerves on fire. "Because I'm curious. And I like collecting things that piss Kane off."

Sariah hesitated, forcing herself to weigh the gamble with every second she could spare. She could keep running blind, exhausted and outnumbered, hoping to throw off Kane and his pack with little more than her wit and luck. Or she could take Ronan's offer. A risk for sure, but not an impossible one if she kept her guard. What game was he playing? She didn't buy the carefree act for a moment. He had a plan — he always did. So which was the greater danger? Kane, relentless and furious, or Ronan with his motives buried behind that easy grin?

She needed time to plan, to patch her wounds, to turn this hunt back against the Alpha. And maybe, just maybe, Ronan knew enough about Kane to make this partnership worth the gamble. To make sure she came out on top when the time came.

With a quiet curse, she jerked her chin. "Fine. Lead the way."

Ronan's safehouse was tucked between two abandoned buildings, barely noticeable unless you knew where to look. Inside, it was surprisingly intact. Dusty, but stocked. A worn couch, a wooden table covered in scattered papers, and a fire pit in the corner, still smoldering from earlier.

Sariah moved cautiously, scanning for exits, weapons, anything that might be a trap.

Ronan lounged on the couch like a king on his throne, lazy and dangerous. He watched her like she was already his favorite new toy. "Relax. If I wanted you dead, I wouldn't have bothered bringing you here."

"That supposed to make me trust you?" she shot back.

"No," he admitted, kicking his feet up. "But you're bleeding, and I'd rather you not ruin my floor."

She glanced down. A deep scratch ran along her forearm, courtesy of her earlier escape. She hadn't even noticed it through the adrenaline.

With a sigh, she sat at the edge of the table as Ronan grabbed a cloth and a bottle of something strong. He knelt in front of her, close enough that she caught the scent of him — smoke and something sharp, like the edge of a blade.

"Hold still, love. This'll hurt." Then, without warning, he poured the liquor over the wound.

Sariah hissed, fingers tightening into fists, but Ronan only chuckled. "Tough girl."

She glared. "Keep talking and I'll bury this knife in your ribs just to see if you still smile."

Ronan smirked but said nothing, methodically wrapping her arm with surprising gentleness. When he finished, he sat back on his heels, eyes unreadable.

"So," he mused, "what did you do to get Kane all riled up?"

Sariah debated lying. But Ronan wasn't stupid, and playing games with him felt like playing chess against someone who already knew your next move.

"Broke into his mansion."

Ronan whistled low. "Ballsy."

She shrugged. "Didn't know it was his."

"And yet you're still breathing. Curious." He leaned in, voice dropping just a fraction. "What is it about you that made the big bad Alpha hesitate?"

Sariah's throat went dry. She looked away.

"Like I said—not your business."

Ronan chuckled, dark and knowing. "Fair enough."

He stood, stretching lazily. "You should rest. I have a feeling Kane won't be far behind, and if you want to stay ahead of him, you'll need your strength."

Sariah didn't argue. She didn't trust him, but right now? She didn't have much of a choice.

As she curled up near the fire, dagger in hand, Ronan watched her from the shadows, his smirk lingering long after she closed her eyes.

She thought she was safe.

6

Chapter 5

The city stank of blood, filth, and *her*.

Kane prowled the maze-like streets of Duskhaven, his pack a living shadow in his wake, a force of nature that parted the night. The howls of distant fights and snarls of rival gangs were nothing compared to the drumbeat in his mind, a rhythm that echoed one thing: lioness. Her scent had wrapped around him the moment they entered the district, a sharp tease that lingered in every corner, always just out of reach. It was under his skin now. A sickness. A fever. Her scent coiled through his blood, an infection that burned hotter with every breath.

Sariah.

She was close. He felt it in his teeth, in his pulse, in the animal part of him that whispered, find her, take her, never let her go. She was close. She had to be.

Beside him, Luka matched his relentless pace, a silent arrow cutting through the foggy streets. Kane knew his Beta was biding his time before he spoke: waiting, watching, calculating the right moment to bare his teeth. Luka's silence was a loaded gun, and Kane felt its weight as they pushed further into the city, each turn closing a noose around the lioness. He was ready for it when

Luka finally pulled the trigger.

"You're losing them." Luka's voice was soft. Dangerous. "They see it. They smell it."

Kane didn't respond or slow his steps as they moved into a territory riddled with danger. Challenges, he thought. Always challenges. His grip on the pack had never been questioned — not until Sariah. She'd changed everything, the way she clawed into his life and twisted the rules. Her defiance set a blaze among his wolves, a whisper of weakness that spread like wildfire. But Kane knew better. It wasn't weakness. It was hunger. A hunger they would never understand. A hunger he couldn't ignore.

"They're waiting, Kane. Watching. Wondering if it's time for something new," Luka continued. "Why you're so set on chasing her. Why a single lioness is worth taking us this deep into enemy territory."

Kane stopped walking. Slowly, he turned his head, leveling Luka with a look that would have sent most men crawling. But Luka wasn't most men. He held his ground.

"I don't explain myself to them," Kane said, voice low, dangerous.

Luka tilted his head. "You don't have to. But wolves challenge weakness. And whether you admit it or not, this—" He gestured to the dark streets, to the search, to the tension thrumming through the pack like a wound ready to tear open. "They think you've forgotten who you are."

Kane didn't need this shit right now. He was on the verge of a growl when Luka called him out, on the verge of a blow, on the verge of caving in skulls and ripping out throats to silence those whispers of doubt. Weakness? He almost laughed. The truth was, he hadn't cut loose in weeks. Maybe that was the problem. Tension coiled tight under his scarred skin, and he welcomed it, fed off it, a beast starved for release. This was what happened when he waited too long to taste blood. Before Kane could spit the words back at his Beta, movement bristled at the edge of his vision. Not just movement—a scent, foreign and wrong in a way that set his instincts ablaze. It wasn't Sariah. But it was trouble.

Kane smelled sweat, steel, and the stink of fear. The moment the first bastard moved, Kane was already on him. The fucker barely had time to blink before Kane caught him out of the air, one brutal swing sending his spine cracking against the pavement. A wet, ugly noise. The wolf beneath him was still alive enough to choke out a single, pitiful gasp before Kane buried his claws into his chest and ripped. He watched the light flicker out of the wolf's eyes, the blood pool black beneath broken ribs and bared teeth. Good. He needed this. He needed more.

Around them, chaos erupted like a bomb. The Rooks. The bastards had been waiting. Kane found himself smiling, a feral curve of lips that barely resembled anything human. He let the violence wash over him, a red haze that drowned out everything but the sound of snarls and screams, the scent of blood, and the bone-deep knowledge that this was what he was made for. They thought he'd grown weak, chasing after Sariah, chasing after something that wasn't revenge and wasn't war. He would show them how wrong they were. Beside him, the night fractured as more shifters poured from the alleys, blades swinging, weapons flashing, teeth and claws bared in a brutal frenzy. Kane's wolves met them head-on, a snarling, violent mass of bodies colliding in the street like an explosion.

Kane was already moving, a force of nature that demolished anything in its path. He tore into the nearest Rook, fist shattering the bastard's jaw before snapping his neck. Another mistake. Kane let him come, let him believe he had an opening. Then he spun—fast, merciless—and cracked the bastard's ribs with one swing of his fist. The wolf dropped, choking on his shattered lungs. One strike to the ribs. Another to the throat. Kane didn't stop moving, didn't stop ripping through them. He was blood and instinct, a storm in motion. By the time the Rook hit the ground, he was already dead.

The street lit up, muzzle flashes piercing the dark as a few of the Rooks drew guns. They were reckless, desperate, catching some of their own in the hail of bullets. Kane ducked low and charged, using the cover of bleeding bodies and the chaos of the fight to close the distance. One of the gunmen saw him late and paled, his eyes wide as Kane reached him, disarmed him, and drove his knife deep into his gut. The shifter convulsed, weapon falling limp from his hand as Kane pulled the blade upward, opening him from belly to throat. He was dead before he hit the ground.

A Rook lunged at him, blade slashing across Kane's ribs. Kane barely felt it. He grabbed the bastard responsible, drove him face-first into the nearest wall, and sank his teeth into his throat. Hot blood spilled over his tongue, metallic and intoxicating.

Another enemy came at him from behind. Kane didn't turn—he just reached back, caught the bastard by the arm, and tore it clean from his socket.

A scream. A wet thud. The scent of death was thick in the air.

The fight didn't last long. It never did.

When the last of the Rooks lay broken in the gutter, Kane stood over the bodies, chest heaving, blood dripping from his hands. He felt his pack's eyes on him. Watching. Measuring.

Good. Let them remember who the fuck he was.

Luka wiped blood from his jaw and exhaled. "Well. That's one way to make a point."

Kane turned to face his pack, eyes burning like embers in the dark. "Anyone else questioning my focus?" His words shot through the night, a challenge wrapped in deadly promise. A dare for anyone to step up and test him. For a long moment, the only sound was the drip of blood from his fingers and the heavy breaths of wolves who knew better than to speak. Silence. He watched them, watched the way they gauged him, their Alpha, lethal and unyielding. And yet he could still feel it under their hard stares. The lingering unease. The tension that hadn't quite faded beneath the bruise-dark night. This wasn't over. No amount of blood would satisfy the whispers gnawing at his heels. Not unless he ended it first. Not unless he gave them the proof they needed, the kind only a dead lioness could provide. He knew those looks, knew the wolves behind them. Knew that what waited in the shadows was a challenge to his command. They might not challenge him now, but they would. Maybe not today or tomorrow. But soon.

Unless he ended it first and ripped the threat apart before it could sink its claws any deeper. That meant finding her. Sariah wasn't just some rogue lioness. She was worse. She was a threat. A distraction. A weakness. A sickness. A fucking infection that no amount of blood could burn away. Why did the thought of catching her make his pulse thunder harder than any hunt? Why, when he should be thinking of her throat beneath his teeth, did he only think of his teeth on her skin?

It was more than a hunt. More than just stalking his prey. When he caught her scent, it wasn't instinct that kicked in. It was something else. Something that made him remember the first time he'd seen her. The first time she'd clawed her way into his life and ruined everything.

7

Chapter 6

Sariah knew she should walk away.

The safehouse was quiet, the fire burning low, casting flickering shadows across the walls. Ronan had stayed close all night, offering warmth, a slow smile, and the kind of easy charm that made it hard to remember he was dangerous.

She should have left already.

Instead, she let herself stay.

"You keep looking at the door," Ronan murmured, pouring dark amber liquid into a glass. "Yet here you are."

Sariah leaned against the wooden table, watching him. "Maybe I'm just waiting for the right moment."

Ronan watched her over the rim of his glass, eyes dark, patient. Like he was waiting for her to step straight into his web. "Or maybe," he said, voice velvet-smooth, "you just don't want to be alone tonight."

She took the drink and let the heat of it burn its way down her throat. Ronan's eyes stayed on her, too knowing, too sharp. He was playing a game.

But so was she.

"You're the kind of trouble people don't walk away from, aren't you?" she mused.

Ronan stepped in, slow and deliberate, until the space between them was nothing. "Only if you want me to be."

His fingers brushed along the inside of her wrist, tracing a barely-there touch that sent an unwanted shiver down her spine.

She should stop this. She should push him away.

But Kane's growl still echoed in her head. Her body still thrummed with restless, tangled frustration.

And Ronan—Ronan was offering an escape.

So when he tilted his head, when his lips ghosted just over hers, she didn't pull away.

The moment their mouths met, it was war.

Sariah didn't ease into it—she tried to take control. But Ronan? Ronan made her fight for it. Her hands fisted in Ronan's shirt, dragging him into her, lips clashing, teeth scraping. He let her. He let her control it, let her yank him down onto the worn couch, let her climb over him like she was the one setting the pace.

But she wasn't stupid.

Ronan might be letting her lead, but he was guiding her the entire time. A shift of his hips here, a slow drag of his nails down her spine there, teasing her with just enough restraint to make her burn.

She hated how well he read her.

She tore at his shirt, dragging her nails down his bare chest as she straddled his lap. He hissed, but the smirk never left his face. "Feisty," he murmured, voice rough now. "You think you're the one in control here?"

Sariah cut him off with another kiss, rolling her hips against him. His fingers dug into her thighs, bruising, but he didn't try to take over. Not yet.

Her teeth sank into his lip, and he laughed—a dark, wicked sound—like she'd done exactly what he wanted.

In one fluid motion, Ronan twisted, flipping her onto her back. The breath whooshed out of her, and before she could react, his mouth was on her throat, teeth scraping, biting, claiming.

"Is this what you needed, little lion?" he rasped against her skin, his hands pinning hers above her head.

Her growl was cut off by a sharp gasp as he rolled his hips against her, pressing into the heat between her thighs. He was teasing her.

Bastard.

Sariah wrenched a hand free, grabbing the back of his neck and dragging him back to her mouth. She could feel him grinning against her lips, cocky, smug. But when she raked her nails down his back hard enough to leave red welts, he shuddered.

Good.

Clothes disappeared between rough kisses and harsh hands. His body was all lean muscle, sharp angles, and wicked intent. He dragged his teeth over her collarbone, nipped at the sensitive skin between her ribs, fingers teasing but never quite giving.

She cursed him. He laughed.

"You can't just take," he murmured against her stomach, pressing a slow, open-mouthed kiss to her hip. "You have to give a little, too."

Sariah's patience snapped. She yanked him back up by his hair, lips crashing against his as she wrapped her legs around him. "Then shut up and do it."

He didn't make her wait any longer.

The first thrust stole her breath, stretching her open as her nails sank into his shoulders.

There was nothing slow or sweet about it. It was raw, fast, deep. His hands locked onto her hips, dragging her back into every brutal snap of his hips, his breath ragged against her ear.

"Fuck, you feel good," he groaned, voice shaking with restraint he was already starting to lose.

Sariah couldn't think, couldn't breathe—only feel. Heat curled low and tight, her body on the edge of something sharp and devastating.

His mouth was everywhere; her jaw, her throat, her chest, his teeth scraping like he wanted to mark her. His fingers slid between them, teasing, pushing her higher, taunting her.

"Come for me," he whispered against her skin, his voice a wicked promise.

She shattered, her body locking tight, pleasure crashing through her so hard she almost saw stars. Ronan followed a moment later, cursing against her mouth as he buried himself deep, shuddering as he spilled inside her.

Sariah should have known better.

She did know better.

Ronan had trouble stitched into every sharp-edged smile, every lazy drawl of his words, every flicker of amusement that never quite reached his eyes. He played games. He was a game. And somehow, she had let herself be maneuvered right into the palm of his hand.

The safehouse was dimly lit, the fire throwing jagged shadows across the room. Sariah sat stiffly on the edge of a battered wooden table, her arms crossed as Ronan poured a generous measure of amber liquid into two glasses. He handed one to her without ceremony.

She scoffed, tipping the glass against her lips again. "You think a couple of drinks and a warm bed means I trust you?"

Ronan smirked, dark and knowing. "Trust me? No. But you do want something from me. You just don't want to admit it yet."

Sariah swallowed the retort on her tongue. He wasn't wrong. She was still running, still hunted, still tangled in a mess she didn't understand. And Ronan? He was the only one offering something instead of demanding it.

Her fingers curled around the glass. "Maybe I just wanted a drink."

He chuckled. "Maybe."

But then he stood, smooth as sin, closing the distance between them in a single unhurried stride. He took the glass from her hand, setting it aside before placing his palms on either side of the table, caging her in without touching her. His breath was warm, whiskey-laced, but his eyes were sharp as a blade against her throat.

"Or maybe," he murmured, "you wanted to know what it would feel like."

The air between them shifted—a snap of tension, something heavy, something unseen threading between them like an invisible snare. Sariah's skin prickled, her body humming with a sensation she did not like.

She moved—to stand, to push him back—but Ronan moved faster. He caught her wrist just as the shift in the air solidified, just as something deep inside her clicked into place.

Her breath seized. Heat licked up her spine, wrapping around her ribs like chains.

No. No, no, no...

Her head snapped up.

Ronan had gone completely still.

The smirk was gone. The easy, teasing mask he wore like armor? Gone.

Sariah's pulse roared in her ears. Her fingers burned where he touched her. An echo of something ancient, something binding, something final vibrated beneath her skin.

Ronan's grip loosened a fraction—but he didn't let go.

His pupils dilated, his breath shallowed, and his throat bobbed in a slow, careful swallow. "Well, fuck."

Sariah ripped her arm back, but it was too late.

The damage was done.

Something tethered her to him now. Not just awareness, not just attraction—something deeper. A pulse at the back of her skull, a new thread in her senses that wasn't there before.

Sariah felt him.

And worst of all? She could tell he felt her too.

Ronan exhaled slowly, rubbing his jaw as his expression shifted. Not cocky now, not even smug, just knowing.

He chuckled, low and dark. "Well, sweetheart. Looks like you walked right into my trap after all."

Her hands clenched into fists. He knew.

Sariah lunged. Claws bared, heart hammering, she struck, but Ronan caught her wrist again, twisting it just enough to turn her attack into nothing.

And then—

A spark. A pulse of something dangerous through the bond.

Sariah choked on a breath, her knees almost buckling as heat flooded her limbs, raw and unwanted, a side effect she hadn't been prepared for.

Ronan's grip tightened just slightly, and she felt it; not just the physical hold, but the way his presence had stitched itself into her own. The weight of him in her senses, the sharp curl of amusement threading through his mind that did not belong to her.

Oh, gods.

The realization clawed through her, ice water down her spine.

He didn't just bond her.

He did it on purpose.

Her pulse slammed against her ribs. "You bastard—"

Ronan grinned, utterly pleased with himself.

"You're welcome."

Her lips curled back in a silent snarl. She needed to get rid of this. Fast. And that meant finding someone in Duskhaven who knew how to sever a bond. "Bonds don't just snap into place," she muttered under her breath. "They require intent. Consent. Magic. A ritual, for gods' sake." She shoved past a pair of startled merchants. "You don't just 'accidentally' bond someone. That bastard knew *exactly* what he was doing." Bonds weren't to be taken lightly. Bonding without a ritual wasn't just unheard of, it was supposed to be impossible. You had to be willing. You had to *choose*. She'd heard whispers as a child—stories of gods forging bonds without consent, without ritual. Twisted things. Cursed things. She'd thought they were just myths. With Ronan's trickery still burning in her veins, Sariah stormed toward the black market, ready to trade stolen goods for information.

She didn't know yet that she was walking into another trap.

She didn't know yet that Darian was waiting.

She thought Ronan's bond was the worst mistake she'd made tonight.

She thought she could fix this.

She thought one bond was bad enough. She had no idea.

33

8

Chapter 7

The black market pulsed like a living beast, its veins choked with stolen goods, whispered deals, and the stink of desperation. Duskhaven's underbelly stretched deep beneath the city like a festering wound, hidden from the eyes of those too weak or too rich to stomach its truths.

It was a place where fortunes were made in blood and souls were bartered for a price.

Tonight, Sariah was desperate enough to pay it.

She moved fast, her hood pulled low, every nerve still burning from Ronan's betrayal. The bastard had played her like a master, and now his claim slithered in the back of her mind, a bond she had never wanted but couldn't tear free from.

Sariah had stepped into dangerous territory before, but this was different.

The air was thick with incense, sweat, and the cloying scent of desperation. She moved through the labyrinth of stalls with purpose, her mind sharp despite the unwanted, lingering hum of Ronan's bond curling at the edges of her awareness.

She needed someone who could sever it.

She needed out.

And Darian? Darian was the only broker with enough venom to cut deep.

She found him exactly where she expected, lounging near the back of the market, draped in shadows, his green eyes glinting like a serpent waiting for something foolish enough to come close.

Sariah stopped a few feet away, arms crossed. "I need a deal."

Darian didn't move. He only tilted his head, studying her. Then, slowly, he stood.

"Do you?" His voice was quiet. Controlled. A blade disguised as silk.

She didn't like the way he was watching her. Not like a threat — worse. Like he already knew something she didn't.

Sariah forced herself to hold his gaze. "I need a bond severed. Fast."

A beat of silence.

Then a slow, creeping smile. Wrong. Too knowing. Too amused.

"Oh?" Darian's voice barely shifted, but Sariah felt the change in the air. "Whose bond, little lion?"

She clenched her jaw. "Not yours, so it doesn't concern you."

Darian exhaled sharply, a quiet chuckle that sent something unpleasant down her spine. Then, with the kind of speed that didn't belong to men, his fingers snapped around her wrist.

Sariah inhaled sharply, ready to yank away, ready to fight—

But the moment his skin touched hers, everything changed.

The black market, the incense, the noise, it all disappeared.

The air between them fractured. The world narrowed. Something unseen snapped tight, yanking like an unseen thread between them.

Sariah gasped, her heart slamming into her ribs.

No. No, no, no—

Darian's entire body locked up. His pupils contracted to slits, his grip tightening on her wrist as if he wanted to let go but physically couldn't.

And then—

He whispered, "No."

Not to her.

To the bond.

His grip turned from a hold to a vice, his breath coming in sharp, barely-contained snarls, his expression collapsing into something she had never seen before.

Darian—cold, unflappable, the man who played power like a game of chess—
Was afraid.

And then Sariah moved.

Without thinking. Without deciding.

Her body just moved, sliding free like it already knew the way. No hesitation. No thought. Just motion. Then—she landed, low and ready. Balanced. Primed to strike.

It was Ronan's.

She knew it the second she felt her weight perfectly distributed, the way her fingers flexed like she was already calculating pressure points, the way her breath was measured, even.

Darian's eyes narrowed slightly. He saw it too.

His jaw tensed, his grip tightening into a fist. "Where the hell did you learn to move like that?"

Sariah swallowed hard. "I—"

She didn't get the chance to finish.

Because suddenly, Darian moved, and this time, she didn't dodge.

Instead, she reacted exactly as he would.

Her foot slid forward, not retreating but advancing, her body turning at just the right angle to cut off a path before he could even take it. She moved without thought—like instinct that wasn't hers had taken the reins.

The second it happened, Darian froze.

The tension in the air shifted.

His breathing slowed, his expression carefully, dangerously blank.

Sariah's pulse pounded, but she wasn't sure if it was her adrenaline or his cold precision creeping through her mind.

Darian's lips parted slightly, his voice a fraction softer. "Oh, you are going to be a problem."

Sariah barely swallowed the lump in her throat. "No one ever said this was part of the bond."

"Because it isn't." Darian's gaze burned into hers, furious, calculating, shaken to his core. "No one... no one's ever done that."

"That's not a bond. That's a fucking theft."

"You took something. That's not how it works."

She didn't just bond to Darian.

She took something from him.

And if it happened with him...

Had it already happened with Ronan?

"This isn't just two bonds." Her breath hitched. "This is something else."

She looked up—and saw the fear still in Darian's eyes.

Not of her.

Of what she might become.

9

Chapter 8

Sariah staggered through The Maw, her vision blurring at the edges.

Darian's venom was a slow, creeping rot in her veins, her body turning against itself in sluggish betrayal. She felt wrong. Her balance was off, her limbs weren't listening, and the world tilted at odd angles, her depth perception shot to hell. Fuck. She'd underestimated how strong his poison was. It wasn't just slowing her down: it was disconnecting her from herself. Sariah stumbled through the labyrinth of filthy streets, forcing herself to move. The air was heavy and wet, clinging to her skin like a predator's breath, and every step felt like wading through tar. Her heart beat a frantic, erratic rhythm against the cold lethargy creeping over her. Damn the snake. The night was too quiet. That was the only warning she got.

She barely dodged a broken crate in the alley, her shoulder slamming into the brick wall instead of missing it. Every step felt like running through wet concrete.

Not now. Not now.

The silence pressed in. The kind that meant predators were close. A shadow moved—then another. Predators.

The scent hit her next, feral, unwashed, edged with hunger. Then the whispers. Too many. The laughter came slow and mean, curling like smoke around her. "Look at this," a voice rasped. "Pretty little lioness. Alone."

Sariah forced herself to stop moving. If she ran now, she'd stumble. If she stumbled, they'd be on her like vultures picking at a corpse.

Her vision swayed. Six of them. Maybe more. They circled her like sharks, their silhouettes blurring in the venom-haze. Three wolves, a jackal, a hyena, and one she couldn't place. Their eyes gleamed too bright in the dim alley, all fangs and easy confidence. They saw the weakness. Smelled it.

One of the wolves, a lanky bastard with scars down his throat, grinned.

"Lost, little lion?"

Sariah curled her claws into her palms, trying to force feeling back into her fingers. Her muscles weren't responding fast enough. Her heartbeat was all wrong—slow in some moments, too fast in others. She needed control. She needed—

The lead wolf lunged.

She barely twisted away in time, but her movements were sluggish, her claws coming out a second too late. She should've torn into his ribs. Instead, she clipped his arm, drawing only a shallow scratch before he was on her again, grabbing a fistful of her vest and yanking her forward.

A knife flashed.

She moved on instinct, jerking to the side, but the blade still ripped along her ribs, slicing through leather and skin alike. Burning pain. The snarl of satisfaction from the wolf's throat rattled inside her skull.

They were going to tear her apart.

They saw her hesitation. Saw the struggle.

Grins widened.

They closed in.

Then—

The world exploded.

Something massive slammed into the lead wolf, hitting him like a battering ram. The air cracked with the force of impact as his body went flying, crashing into the alley wall hard enough to leave a dent. The other shifters barely had time to react before the hulking form of a bear barreled into them, scattering bodies like ragdolls.

Torin.

He didn't fight like the others. No grace. No theatrics. Just unrelenting force.

The jackal barely managed to snarl before Torin grabbed him by the throat and slammed him face-first into the pavement. A sharp, wet crunch. The hyena turned to run — Torin caught him by the leg and threw him like a sack of bones, his body bouncing off the alley wall before crumpling.

One of the wolves hesitated, caught between fight and flight.

Torin's stare was an executioner's axe.

The wolf ran.

Torin didn't follow. Didn't even move. He just watched.

Sariah breathed hard, slumping against the wall.

She was alive.

She wasn't sure how the hell that had just happened.

Then Torin turned to her.

Without a word, he crouched, grabbed her under the knees and shoulders, and lifted her like she weighed nothing.

Sariah snapped out of it.

"The hell—" she started, thrashing weakly. "Put me down."

Torin didn't even look at her.

"No."

And just like that, he started walking.

* * *

Sariah woke to the scent of smoke, steel, and sweat.

Her body ached. The venom was fading, but every muscle in her screamed protest as she pushed herself up. She was lying on a cot, wrapped in a thin, too-warm blanket. Blood on the floor. Old. Rust-colored. Stained deep into the stone.

Torin sat across from her, arms folded, watching.

His gaze was steady, impassive. Unreadable.

"Where— " She swallowed hard, voice raw. "Where the hell am I?"

Torin didn't blink.

"Safe."

The word hit her like a blow.

Safe?

She frowned, gaze flicking past him. Reinforced iron walls. A single, flickering light overhead. Beyond the doorway, the faint clang of metal.

An arena.

She knew this place. Torin's underground. A place where blood stained the floors deeper than time could erase.

Her fingers curled into the blanket. It was warm. She was warm.

He had wrapped her in it.

She didn't know what to do with that.

"Why?" she asked finally.

Torin's stare didn't waver.

"You were dying in my streets."

"That doesn't answer the question."

Torin exhaled sharply. Not a sigh. Something closer to frustration.

"If I find a bleeding woman about to be torn apart, I stop it. It's what I do."

She stared at him. "You'd have done that for anyone?"

A long, heavy pause.

Then a single, unwavering nod.

"Yes."

It shouldn't sting.

But it did.

With Kane, Ronan, and Darian, she knew why they wanted her. Motives. Power plays. Obsession.

But Torin?

Torin wanted nothing from her.

And somehow, that was worse.

Sariah exhaled sharply. "Fine. Thanks for the rescue. I'll get out of your way."

She swung her legs off the cot and the world tilted.

Her vision swam.

She was falling.

Torin caught her. Heat. Solid hands on her waist. Steady. Unshakable. She froze. Then—just for a second—she leaned into him. Not desire. Not trust. Just... a moment. A breath of not being alone. There was a tightness in his jaw. Not irritation. Guilt? She yanked herself away. Torin let go immediately, stepping back. Neither of them spoke. Neither of them acknowledged it. It was nothing. Just a moment.

Sariah clenched her jaw. "I'm leaving."

Torin didn't stop her. Sariah shoved through the door and into the night—

But for just a second, she swore she could still feel the heat of his hands.

Not on her skin. In her bones.

But as she left, she felt his eyes on her.

Not like Kane.

Not like Ronan.

Not like Darian.

Torin didn't want anything from her. Not power. Not obedience. Not even thanks.

And somehow... that made him the most dangerous of them all.

Chapter 9

Sariah didn't make it far before she felt it.

The shift in the air. The weight of something hunting her.

She didn't turn around. Didn't need to.

She knew who it was.

And she knew he wouldn't be alone.

Kane had finally found her.

Sariah inhaled through her nose, slow and steady, before pivoting on her heel.

There they were.

Kane at the front, his wolves fanning out behind him. They moved like a unit: silent, coordinated. Predators closing in on a wounded animal.

But Sariah wasn't prey.

She exhaled sharply, glancing past them, past the buildings that led to the underground arena she'd just left.

She could run.

But Kane would go after Torin next.

And for some fucking reason, that didn't sit right with her.

So instead of running, she turned back.

Torin barely reacted when she stormed back into the arena. Just lifted his gaze. Calm. Unmoved. Unshaken.

"They're here," Sariah said, her pulse steady, her stance already bracing for the fight.

Torin didn't ask who.

He already knew.

When Kane's scent finally filled the room, heavy with raw aggression, Torin just rolled his shoulders like he'd been expecting it.

The wolves filed in, but no one spoke.

Not at first.

Because the second Kane laid eyes on her, the entire world shrank down to just the two of them.

His gaze raked over her, nostrils flaring, and Sariah felt it.

That pull.

The thing that had been driving him mad since the moment he caught her.

His jaw clenched, muscles flexing beneath his shirt.

He smelled her now.

Not just her scent.

The scent of another man's territory on her skin.

The growl that ripped from his throat was deep, violent, and fucking murderous.

Sariah braced as Kane's eyes flicked past her to Torin.

Kane's nostrils flared again. His fingers flexed at his sides.

"She's mine."

Torin didn't flinch. Didn't shift. Didn't blink.

He just stood there. Massive and unmoved.

Then, slowly, deliberately, he looked at Sariah. Not at Kane.

"Didn't smell like it."

The room went still.

Sariah's stomach dropped.

The wolves tensed. A few snarls rippled through them, but Kane—

Kane fucking smirked.

Then he lunged.

The first hit cracked the air like a gunshot. Kane slammed into Torin, full force, but the bear didn't budge. Didn't stumble. Didn't even fucking flinch.

Torin swung.

His fist collided with Kane's ribs, sending the Alpha flying into a wall.

Dust and shattered concrete rained down.

Kane snarled, shaking off the impact. Then launched himself forward again.

This time, it was pure carnage.

Torin wasn't fast.

But he didn't need to be.

He fought like an unstoppable force. Every blow heavy enough to shatter bone.

Kane, on the other hand, was all speed and precision. Where Torin tanked hits, Kane dodged and countered, slashing, striking, tearing.

By the time they ripped apart from each other, the entire arena was half-destroyed.

The wolves stood back, waiting. Watching.

Sariah?

She had fucking had enough.

The moment Kane rushed Torin again, Sariah moved.

Fast.

She stepped between them, spun, and kicked Kane straight in the fucking chest. The impact sent him skidding backward, dust rising around his boots as he came to a slow, deliberate stop. When he looked up, he was smiling.

Not the kind of smile that meant peace.

The kind that said she'd just made things more interesting.

Sariah didn't care. She wasn't letting them tear each other apart over her.

She unsheathed her claws, snarling. "Are you done?"

Kane's eyes darkened with something she didn't want to name.

"Not even close."

His wolves shifted behind him, waiting.

Then Kane straightened, rolling his shoulders, and said, "You want to be done? Then make a choice."

Sariah's heartbeat slowed.

"You stole from me," Kane continued, his voice low, rough. "My pack doesn't forgive thieves."

The wolves rumbled in agreement.

"So here's the deal," Kane went on. "You either join my pack and earn your place, or we hunt you like the prey you are."

Silence.

Sariah's stomach twisted.

Not in fear.

In fury.

But Kane wasn't wrong. She'd stolen from him. She'd run. His pack would never accept her unless she proved she belonged. Her claws flexed. She could fight. She could run again. But in the end…

She already knew the answer. She met Kane's gaze, defiant, unyielding.

"I'll come," she said.

Kane's smirk deepened.

"But," she added, lifting her chin, "Torin comes with me."

A ripple went through the wolves.

Kane's expression hardened. "That's not how this works."

"It is now."

She didn't know why she said it.

Didn't know why the thought of leaving Torin behind made her chest tighten.

And she wasn't going to fight that instinct.

Kane stared at her for a long time.

Then, slowly, his gaze shifted to Torin.

The bear didn't speak.

Didn't move.

Just stood there, like a fucking mountain, waiting.

Kane exhaled sharply, gritting his teeth.

Then—he laughed.

A low, dark, almost amused sound.

"Fine," Kane said. "Let's see if you two can survive the den."

And just like that, the game changed.

Forever.

11

Chapter 10

The Howl reeked of wolves that wanted her dead.

Sariah strode in behind Kane, keeping her steps measured and steady, but she felt it. Hostility. Rage.

Kane's wolves lined the walls, watching her like an infection.

She didn't belong here, and the only reason she was still standing was because Kane had brought her in.

But that wasn't enough.

She had to earn her place in blood.

Sariah knew the wolves would demand it.

The moment she stepped into the clearing, the air thickened, charged with the kind of anticipation that only came before a kill. The pack surrounded her in a loose half-circle, every pair of eyes sharp, hungry. Assessing. Weighing.

Kane stood at the center, his arms crossed, his expression unreadable.

"You've made things... complicated," he said, his voice calm but edged with something sharper. Possession. Command. A warning.

Sariah lifted her chin. "That tends to happen when people try to cage me."

A low ripple of amusement stirred through the wolves, but Kane didn't so much as blink. He glanced toward Luka, the same bastard who had been eyeing her like a chew toy since the moment she arrived.

Luka stepped forward, a slow grin stretching across his face.

Sariah's stomach clenched. She already knew where this was going.

Kane's voice was quiet, absolute. "You want to prove you belong? Then fight for it."

Luka cracked his knuckles. "I'll make it easy for you, girl. Stay down when you hit the dirt, and maybe I won't break you too badly."

Sariah huffed a laugh. "How generous."

Luka lunged.

She ducked the first strike, shifting smoothly into a defensive stance. No hesitation. No fear. He was bigger, stronger, but she was faster. Smarter. And she had fought for her life more times than she could count.

The next hit came quicker. She pivoted, but Luka was expecting it. He caught her shoulder, spinning her back hard enough that she nearly lost her footing.

The wolves howled their approval.

Sariah gritted her teeth, shaking off the impact. She wouldn't give them the satisfaction. She wouldn't lose.

Luka smirked. "What's the matter? Not as quick as you thought?"

Sariah wiped blood from her lip and smiled. "You talk too much."

She feinted left, then snapped her elbow up, catching him right in the throat.

Luka gagged, stumbling back. The watching wolves went dead silent for half a second. Then the energy changed, no longer entertained, but interested.

Luka recovered fast, his eyes burning with something darker now. He rolled his shoulders. Serious, now. Ready to kill.

"Bad move," he snarled.

Then he shifted.

His bones snapped, his body morphing mid-lunge, fur exploding from his skin as claws replaced fingers.

Sariah barely had time to react before he was on her, moving twice as fast as before.

She hit the ground hard.

Pain shot up her spine, but she rolled, just avoiding the slice of claws that could have torn her throat open. She kicked out, catching him in the ribs, but it was like kicking solid iron. Too strong. Too fast.

Luka snarled and went for the kill.

Kane's voice cut through the chaos like a blade.

"Enough."

Everything stopped.

Luka froze mid-motion, his fangs inches from her neck. His body trembled with the effort to hold back, to obey.

Sariah's pulse hammered against her ribs, but she refused to look away from Kane.

Slowly, deliberately, he stepped forward. The pack parted for him. He looked down at her, something unreadable in his storm-gray eyes.

He offered her his hand.

Sariah hesitated.

The pack watched. Waiting.

If she took it, she would be making a choice.

If she refused... she might not get another chance.

Her fingers curled, but before she could decide, Kane's voice came again, softer this time.

"Choose, little lion."

Stay a lone wolf, or join the pack.

She swallowed hard, and reached for his hand.

The second they were alone, Kane slammed her against the wall, breath ragged, hands rough.

It wasn't enough. It would never be enough.

Sariah could feel it: his need, his obsession, his unraveling. He grabbed her by the jaw, forcing her to look at him, forcing her to see what she was doing to him.

"You have no idea," he growled, his voice wrecked, shaking, "how fucking long I've needed this."

She smiled.

Slow.

Sharp.

"Then take it."

Kane lost it.

His mouth crashed into hers, teeth, tongue, war. He didn't just kiss, he claimed. Bit. Devoured.

His hands ripped at her clothes, hers tore at his, a frenzy of skin and heat and pure fucking hunger.

Then he was inside her.

Hard. Deep. Brutal.

Sariah arched against him, nails digging into his shoulders, marking him just as he was marking her. The air was thick with their breath, with sweat, with the wild, ragged sound of bodies colliding.

And then she bit him.

Hard.

Kane froze.

His entire body went taut, his muscles locking down, his breath shattering against her skin.

The bond hit.

It was a shockwave, a violent rip through his body. Fire, pain, pleasure, too much, too fucking much.

Kane's grip tightened, his head snapping back, veins bulging in his neck, a guttural snarl tearing from his throat. His entire world was burning.

He felt her inside him.

Her want. Her need. Her fucking power.

She owned him.

Sariah saw it the second he realized. The second his dominance cracked. The second she had him.

And she fucking reveled in it.

She twisted her hips, taking him deeper, watching him break apart beneath her hands.

"You feel that?" she whispered, her lips at his ear, voice dark and sweet. "That's what it feels like to be mine."

Kane snapped.

He grabbed her, hard, desperate, fucking wrecked, and flipped them, slamming her onto the bed.

His hips pistoned forward, brutal and relentless, dragging her into his madness, into the raw, unbearable heat of the bond tearing them apart just as it fused them together.

Sariah clawed at his back, writhing, biting, meeting his brutal pace with one of her own.

Kane was losing himself, his growls rough, his breath shaking. His eyes were wild, feral, locked onto hers like she was the only thing keeping him from coming apart completely.

"You fucking ruined me," he rasped against her throat, biting down, branding her with his teeth.

"I know," Sariah gasped, her nails dragging down his spine, urging him deeper.

Then she tightened around him.

And Kane fell.

His body locked, his hands fisting in the sheets, his groan ripping through the air as he came apart inside her.

With it, the bond sealed.

It was a violent, devastating thing. A tether of heat and hunger and primal fucking need that left no room for anything else.

Kane collapsed against her, his body still shaking. His breath was ragged, his hands still gripping her like he'd never fucking let go.

And when he lifted his head, when he looked at her with those burning, wrecked eyes—

She knew.

He'd never wanted this.

But now, he'd never fucking let her go.

Sariah smirked, brushing her thumb across his bloody lower lip.

"How's that for ruined, Alpha?"

12

Chapter 11

Darian had spent his life mastering control. Words were his weapons, sharper than any blade. Secrets were his currency, more valuable than blood. He had built his world on precision and manipulation, and it had made him untouchable. The king of Serpent's Row. And then she happened, and it all went to hell.

The second the bond snapped into place, it had been a noose. A sickness. A mistake. One heartbeat, they were nothing; the next, he was tied to her by threads he couldn't break, as if his very bones were shackled. The bond thrummed, and he could feel Ronan's claim on her, painted across his skin like words carved to wound. That had been insufferable enough. But then Kane. Darian had felt everything.

Sariah surrendering. Letting Kane own her, ruin her, fuck her into submission. The bond didn't just show him. It made him feel it. The hunger, the need. The pure, unrestrained ecstasy of it. It opened him in ways he'd never known, hollowed him out and filled him with something raw and primal, and it had driven him fucking mad.

In Serpent's Row, everything had a price, and Darian was willing to pay it. He couldn't go on like this, couldn't stand the loss of control that battered him every second she was with Kane or Ronan, the humiliation of wanting what he couldn't have, of craving with no way to satisfy it. The bond was like an infection spreading through him. He only had to survive until she broke, until he was the only one left, but until then, he needed the madness to stop.

Darian had gone to the only power in Duskhaven worse than him. Desperation clawed at him, driving him through the mists and alleys of The Veil, through shadows that swallowed him whole. A dark sorcerer. A nightmare in human skin. One whispered about with fear and reverence, spoken of only in secrets and half-truths. But Darian knew where to find him. There wasn't a corner of Duskhaven he couldn't reach, not a single place beyond his grasp, and when he had stormed into the sorcerer's lair, he'd found exactly what he expected: a chill that sunk into the soul, an air heavy with the weight of ancient curses. He'd also found a resolve that grated against every nerve in his body.

"Sever the bond," Darian had said, voice ragged, unsteady. "I don't care what it takes." What he hadn't expected was the knowing look, the smirk that made his insides coil. The sorcerer had just smiled, as if Darian's suffering was an old friend.

"You don't want it gone," he murmured, his voice like smoke snaking through the air. "You just don't want to feel it."

Darian's hands curled into fists, his blood boiling beneath skin that was once ice-cold. "Do it." The command was a growl, a plea, an agony he couldn't hide. He hated how raw it sounded, how close to breaking it seemed.

The sorcerer had hummed, fingers tracing lazy symbols in the air. Dark tendrils seemed to follow his gestures, and Darian had felt a flicker—a momentary glimpse into what he wanted most.

"I need her."

The words had been a dagger, sharp and precise, cutting through the thin fabric of Darian's control. He had stiffened, the movement instinctual, the reaction as much anger as it was fear. The sorcerer's eyes had gleamed, catching the dim light like polished onyx.

"Her blood. Her presence. Then I'll take it away."

Darian's stomach twisted, a serpent turning over on itself. He was used to the duplicity of deals, the viciousness of bargaining in Duskhaven, but this—this was too close, too much. He had come to free himself, to burn away the chains that Sariah had wrapped around him. But she was in this, too, in the solution like she was in the problem, and it was a cruel irony he couldn't stand. She was the center of everything, even now, even here, where her neck was not on the line beside his. Or maybe it was.

His mind spiraled, caught in the web of what ifs and can I, and in a sickening instant the truth hit him: he hadn't expected this cost. It hadn't occurred to him that he couldn't pay it, wouldn't pay it. The panic swept through him, fraying his thoughts, loosening the edges of his confidence.

Because for the first time since the bond had formed, he hesitated.

But the memory came back.

Kane. His hands on her. His mouth on her. The way she fucking melted for him.

Darian's jaw clenched.

"Fine."

Sariah came to him like a fool. She thought she was meeting an informant. She should have known better. The second she stepped into the darkened alley, Darian moved.

He grabbed her, spun her, and slammed her into the wall.

She snarled, claws flashing, until her gaze landed on his.

Her expression shifted.

Not to fear.

To anger.

"You."

Darian's stomach tightened.

"Did you miss me, little lion?" he murmured, his fingers digging into her wrists.

Sariah bared her teeth. "Go fuck yourself."

Darian almost laughed. She smelled like Kane. Like sex. Like submission. Like she had given herself over completely.

The bond inside him throbbed.

He fucking hated it.

"You shouldn't have come alone," he said, voice too even.

Sariah stiffened.

A second too late.

Because hands grabbed her from the shadows.

And then she was dragged away.

Darian watched it happen.

Watched as the sorcerer's men bound her wrists, gagged her mouth.

Watched as her eyes locked onto his, full of rage, betrayal.

She struggled, snarled, fought. But the magic was already sinking into her skin, making her body weak, unresponsive.

The bond twisted.

Darian's breath hitched.

Something tightened in his chest.

The bond loosened.

It was a whisper of release, a cruel tease of freedom.

A breath of air after weeks of drowning.

And Darian hated it.

His hands curled into fists. His breath hitched. Something inside him tore.

The bond had been suffocating, unbearable, a cage that crushed him.

And now that it was fading—

He wanted to claw it back.

The sorcerer watched him, smiling like he had seen this a thousand times before. Like he knew exactly what Darian was feeling.

"Strange, isn't it?" The sorcerer's voice was almost gentle. Mocking. "How you've spent so much time trying to rid yourself of her, only to realize you can't live without her?"

Darian's jaw clenched. He would not react. He would not show weakness.

But his vision blurred.

His hands shook.

His body was rejecting this.

Sariah.

He could feel her slipping through his fingers. The raw, burning wrongness of it. The bond wasn't severed, not yet. But it was hanging by a thread, and it was taking pieces of him with it.

He was coming apart.

And she knew it.

Sariah fucking knew.

She didn't scream. Didn't beg. She only watched him.

And she smiled.

Not in fear.

Not in anger.

In triumph.

Her lips parted, her voice a whisper of cruel satisfaction.

"How does it feel?"

Darian's stomach twisted.

Sariah tilted her head, her gaze piercing through him. Through his control. Through the careful walls he had built around himself.

"How does it feel," she whispered, "to finally lose me?"

His world tilted.

It was working. The bond was breaking. The thing he had begged for, bled for, hunted for.

And he wanted to rip it apart with his bare hands.

He had fucked up.

He had fucked up so badly.

The sorcerer stepped forward, brushing a finger over Sariah's jaw. "You should thank your mate," he murmured. "He's the reason you're here."

Sariah didn't flinch. She only held Darian's gaze and twisted the blade deeper.

"Goodbye, snake."

They dragged her into the dark.

And Darian felt it.

The bond stretched, frayed, pulled taut like a rope ready to snap. His lungs seized. His knees almost buckled.

He should have been relieved.

Instead, he had never been more terrified in his fucking life.

The last thing he heard was her laughter.

She was gone.

The bond was almost gone.

And Darian was breaking.

13

Chapter 12

The second Darian stepped into The Howl, the wolves were on him.

No words. No warning.

The first hit caught him in the ribs, knocking the breath from his lungs.

The second one? Straight to the jaw.

The third? That was Kane.

And after that, Darian stopped counting.

He let them take him down. Didn't raise a hand. Didn't flinch. He let them knock every breath from his lungs, drag him through the dirt like an animal. He deserved this. Deserved worse for what he'd done. The first hit burst the side of his face, blood already trickling down his neck, warm and sticky. The next had sent stars through his vision. Darcy was the one who caught him solid in the gut. Axel hit him low, and Dixon kicked his legs from under him. One after another, a blur of fists and feet, boot strikes that took every ounce of fight from him. He knew the wolves wouldn't stop until they had their fill. Until Kane called them off. They carried him through the dirt, the stink of sweat and fur in his nose. This was what he came for. What he needed. What he owed. They held him up, barely keeping him standing.

And there, waiting, was Kane.

The Alpha sat in his usual chair but he wasn't lounging. This time, he was coiled like a striking snake. His elbows rested on his knees, hands clasped like he was holding something in. The old Kane would have been relaxed, feasting on the show. Not anymore. Not with Darian. Not like this.

But his eyes.

His eyes were death.

Darian coughed blood, straightened his spine, and met the gaze of the man who was about to kill him. He'd let that happen too. It was what he came for.

Kane exhaled slowly and tilted his head.

"Well." His voice was quiet. Too quiet. "You look like shit."

The pack laughed. A few shoved Darian, egging Kane on. They wanted more. More pain, more punishment. More than Kane usually dished out. Kane let them have their fun, ignoring their taunts, watching Darian like he was the only thing in the room.

And when he stood, the laughter stopped.

Kane didn't need speed. He didn't need showmanship. He was death. And death moved at its own pace.

Darian didn't resist when Kane's hand wrapped around his throat and lifted him clean off the ground. Didn't struggle when his back hit the wall hard enough to crack stone. Didn't even try to breathe. Blood dripped from his mouth, sliding over Kane's knuckles.

Kane leaned in, nose to nose, his voice a whisper of pure violence.

"Give me one reason I shouldn't rip your fucking throat out right now."

Darian swallowed, tasting blood.

"Sariah's gone."

The world stopped.

Kane's fingers tightened.

Too tight.

Darian felt something in his neck shift. He had seconds before Kane lost control completely.

"I —" Darian choked, forcing it out, feeling his own blood bubble up. "I gave her to the sorcerer."

Kane snapped the truth in Darian's words cut too close to the bone, the failure too raw to endure. His first punch shattered the promise of control, broke the last thread restraining his rage. It broke something else too, in Darian's shoulder or chest. Darian didn't know, couldn't tell. His vision swam with blood and black dots, his ears ringing with the echo of Kane's fury. The second strike? That made the ringing unbearable, a high-pitched whine that swallowed the other sounds around him. The third, fourth, fifth? He lost count. Lost sensation. He stopped feeling them altogether, his world reduced to the taste of copper and the agony of nothingness. Kane's fist was a relentless storm, a cyclone of violence that crashed into his jaw, his ribs, his gut. A storm of rage that Darian let consume him because he deserved it. Because he needed it like air.

But there was more than just punishment in Kane's blows. Darian could see it, even as the world blurred and slipped away. Kane's snarling grief. He was pummeling the one person who could take it, the one person still standing when Sariah wasn't. Every hit was a second lost, a moment slipping further away. Every punch was an accusation, a scream at himself. You let her go. You should've kept her close. You failed her. Kane raged against himself as much as against Darian, fury churning as he fought to hold on to something already gone. He struck and struck until Darian's bones felt like water and his mind ached from the beating, the whole world a smear of red and regret. Kane yanked Darian's half-unconscious body up and kept him upright just long enough to do even more damage. Kane wanted him to feel it. All of it. But by then? By then Darian couldn't even feel his skin.

He had one thing left.

He had his voice. His regret.

He forced the words out, past the blood.
"Tell Sariah—"
His head dropped.
Kane didn't stop.
"Tell her I'm sorry."
Another hit. Another rib broken.
Darian's vision blurred. He wasn't coming back from this. Kane had killed men for less. He was going to die here.
A shadow moved.
A voice, low and steady.
"Enough."
Kane's fist stopped. He turned, slowly.
Torin was watching. Not moving. Not threatening.
Just waiting. His gaze held something heavy.
Kane bristled. "You think he deserves to breathe after that?"
Torin tilted his head.
"Maybe not," he said. "But she does."
The words hit like a knife.
Kane's chest heaved. His fingers twitched.
Not Darian.

Sariah.

Kane's hands curled into fists but the fight was gone.

Because Torin was right.

Kane exhaled hard. Wiped the blood from his knuckles.

Looked down at Darian.

"You're coming with us," he growled. "And if you slow us down, I'll kill you myself."

Darian nodded.

Not because he had a choice.

But because he had already decided.

He was never losing her again.

And this time?

He wouldn't hesitate.

14

Chapter 13

Ronan felt it before it happened.

A shift in the air. A fracture in the bond.

Something was wrong.

Not wrong like a fight gone south. Not wrong like bad luck or a botched deal.

Wrong like the world itself was tearing apart.

The thread between him and Sariah had frayed to nothing. Too faint. Too thin. Too far.

And Kane?

Kane was a storm on the verge of snapping its chains.

Darian's agony bled into the night like an open wound. Desperate. Poisonous. A man trying to fix something already shattered.

Torin was waiting.

Silent. Watching. A force of nature on the verge of deciding whether to end this or let it play out. Ronan had to move.

He cut through The Veil like a shadow slipping between cracks, his coat whipping behind him as his boots barely touched the ground.

Duskhaven was a beast with too many teeth, and too many eyes, but he knew every dark corner. Every alley. Every shortcut.

He had to get to The Howl.

He had to get to them.

He shot through the narrow alleys of The Veil like an arrow released from a bow, coat trailing behind him, breath forming clouds in the cold night air. Duskhaven was a labyrinth, but he knew it better than anyone. The city had tried to swallow him over a thousand times, and it had lost every time. His raven eyes darted, sharp with intention, as he wove through the maze of cracked brick and rusted iron. He had to reach The Howl. He had to reach the others.

The second Ronan stepped inside, he knew. The stench of fresh blood choked the air. This wasn't a fight.

This was slaughter.

Wolves stood at the edges of the room, too still. They weren't enjoying this. They were waiting. Kane had gone too far.

Darian was a fucking mess on the floor, Blood everywhere, soaking through his expensive shirt and pooling at his side.

His breathing was ragged.

His eyes unfocused.

Above him, Kane.

His knuckles were raw. Split wide, drenched in blood, his bones bruised from hitting Darian so many fucking times.

His shoulders heaved with every breath; his body strung too tight.

And his eyes.

Not human.

Not even wolf.

Something worse.

Ronan had seen Kane in a thousand fights. Seen him covered in blood, seen him rip a man apart like it was sport, but this? This was different. This was the end of Kane's control.

Torin had taken up position like a silent sentinel, back to the wall, arms crossed over his massive chest. Dense, unmoved, a brooding giant. The kind of force that decided if someone else needed to be torn apart and did so with lethal precision. His hazel eyes flickered, measuring the situation with that quiet intensity, while his presence alone kept the wolves at bay.

Ronan took it all in with a quick, darting glance. The tension. The wreckage. The broken bodies. The sense of things spiraling wildly out of control. Sariah slipping away while the city itself seemed to turn against them. His mind raced even as his voice cut sharply across the room, shattering the thick silence like a knife through flesh.

"Alright." His voice broke the silence like a blade. "What the fuck did I just walk into?"

Kane's golden eyes snapped to him immediately, shards of amber burning with fury. Predatory and merciless.

There was no amusement there. No trace of a cocky grin or a sardonic edge. No hint of control. Only primal rage, wild and untamable as a pack of starving wolves. It threatened to consume them all.

Ronan's trademark smirk faltered. Just for a second, but in that second, he felt the enormity of it, the danger. Because Kane looked only one breath away from murder. One heartbeat from absolute carnage.

But then Ronan's attention shifted.

Darian.

The snake shifter sprawled on the floor, bleeding. He was panting, each breath a wheeze of agony. Ronan could sense the underlying desperation beneath every ragged inhale. The hovering specter of defeat that clung to him like a shadow. But those eyes...

His eyes were wrecked.

Ronan felt a twist of recognition, sharp as a blade. The same brutal loss that slashed through him, the same desperation that clawed. The bond with Sariah slipped like sand through his fingers. The distance grew, stretching into a chasm. A noose tightening, choking off their connection. Her life force bleeding into nothingness.

And suddenly, everything clicked.

Torin was unmoving, waiting, like a sleeping beast that couldn't be roused. Kane was unhinged, a hunter with nothing left to kill. Darian's silent scream of panic, guilt gnawing like the venom of his own bite.

Sariah was dying.

And they couldn't reach her.

Ronan's smirk vanished completely. That self-assured mask drained from his face, leaving the raw edge of panic in its absence. His stomach twisted, coiled with an anxiety that spread like poison through his veins. He looked back at Kane, then at Darian, then at Torin, seeing now what he had failed to see before. The full, terrible truth of it. The bear said nothing. Not a single word.

But Ronan didn't need him to.

He already knew.

The bond was faint. Barely a thread. Kane was feral. A force of rage ready to destroy friend and foe alike. Darian was desperate. Despairing, lost in the ruin of his own making. Torin was waiting. Like a massive, silent avalanche about to fall. And Sariah? Sariah was gone.

Ronan's jaw tightened. His entire body tensed with a furious resolve, muscles rigid and ready to burn this world to ashes to find her. He exhaled slowly, then ran a hand down his face, fighting to hold onto his control. Fighting to stay ahead of a game that was spiraling far beyond his reckoning.

He shouted the question that was ripping him apart, the one that cut through the core of them all like a blade:

"Where the fuck is Sariah?"

It's War.
   Darian just lost everything.
   Kane is ready to kill.
   Torin is ready to move.
   And Ronan just realized they're all about to burn the city down to get her back.

15

Chapter 14

Pain.

That was the first thing Sariah felt. Raw and primal, demanding her attention, splintering through her with no mercy. Not an ache. Not a sting. Not something she could ignore or shove away. Pure, excruciating, soul-deep agony. It claimed her mind, her senses, her very will. Sariah screamed, a ragged sound that tore from her throat, echoing off cold stone walls. Her body jerked against cold iron chains, the metal burning into her wrists and ankles, searing her skin like fire. She was drowning in pain. The air smelled of blood, decay, and something wrong. Wrong, like everything twisted and shattered. She forced her blurry vision to focus.

Stone walls. Faint candlelight. Symbols carved into the floor.

And him.

The sorcerer. Sitting in a chair across from her, watching.

His eyes were sharp, calculating, like she was an experiment, and he was studying a fascinating puzzle, eager to see the pieces fall into place. He smiled. "Ah. You're awake." His voice was low, a smooth taunt. "Though I can't promise for how long."

Sariah snarled, thrashing against the chains, but her limbs failed her. Her body was weak, trembling beneath the effort to break free. She felt something inside herself unraveling, like strings being cut loose, one by one. Her bonds. The fierce and unbreakable connections to her pack: Kane, Ronan, Darian, Torin. They weren't severed. But they were slipping away through her fingers like water. Panic gripped her, fierce and consuming, even as the sorcerer's gaze pinned her like a knife. He tilted his head as if inspecting her.

"Fascinating," he murmured, the words low and cutting. "Four different bonds. And yet, none of them are your kind."

Sariah's breath hitched, the sudden fear even stronger than the agony that still wracked her. She was losing them. Losing everything.

"A wolf. A raven. A bear. A snake."

The words were a taunt and a challenge, each one like an accusation. He leaned forward in his chair, fingers steepled together, his posture that of a predator toying with its prey. "Tell me, little lioness. What is it about you that makes them defy nature?"

His eyes gleamed with the question, glittering with cruel curiosity. Every instinct Sariah possessed screamed at her to fight back, to hold on even as the world slipped further from her grasp. She bared her teeth, a feral sound escaping her lips. "Go to hell."

The sorcerer sighed, one long breath that echoed through the chamber. "Not the answer I was looking for."

He lifted his hand, a lazy, dismissive gesture that sent a chill through her veins. The symbols on the floor flared to life, burning with an unholy light that seared itself into her vision. An incantation, Sariah realized with cold horror; he didn't even need to speak it aloud. Her chains rattled violently as she struggled, her voice rising in a scream that shattered the air like glass.

The pain wasn't physical.

It was worse. More consuming. More savage. Her brain reeled, trying to comprehend. The pain should have been impossible. Yet it wasn't. Her lips peeled back in another choked scream. The pain had changed. Shifted. Became something far more sinister.

It was inside her.

Like splintered shards working through her blood. Like someone had hooked their claws into her soul and was pulling. Sariah thrashed violently, chains rattling. But there was no escape.

Her veins burned as something dark, ancient, unnatural tried to sever the bonds. A force she could not see but felt, crawling through her bones, wrapping like wire around her heart. Panic and terror collided in a brutal wave. The connections to her pack slipped away faster, stretched so thin they felt like they would snap.

Ronan. Kane. Darian. Torin. Their names were a litany in her head, a chant that drowned out the sorcerer's laughter. They fought back.

They clawed and tore into the blackness that tried to claim her. They were fire and rage, unrelenting, refusing to let go. But the assault didn't end. The symbols around her burned with unholy power, cutting deeper and deeper, unraveling her mind.

She was slipping.

Falling into memories.

Or maybe they were reaching for her.

"You have no idea, how fucking long I've needed this."

Kane's hands gripping her hips. Holding her down. Claiming her.

His teeth at her throat, his breath hot, ragged, wrecked.

She could feel his obsession, his hunger, his need to consume her.

Her chest tightened.

Where was he now?

She tried to call for him.

But there was only darkness.

"You really think you're the one in control here?"

Ronan's smirk. The way his fingers danced along her skin, teasing, taunting.

His voice, velvet-smooth. His laugh, soft and knowing.

Ronan had tricked her. Bound her first.

And now?

Now his bond was fading.

Sariah felt it slipping away —

And it terrified her.

"You shouldn't have come alone."

Darian's voice in her head.

His betrayal a knife between her ribs.

But now she felt his panic.

He had felt the bond loosen too.

And for the first time, Darian was afraid.

Not of losing the bond.

Of losing her.

Torin had never spoken about the bond.

Never claimed her.

But in her haze, she felt him.

A steady presence, unmoving.

A force she had leaned into without realizing.

Her fingers curled.

She wasn't ready to lose him either.

The bonds were fading.

But they weren't breaking.

She wouldn't let them.

Sariah clenched her jaw, sucking in a ragged breath, and focused, Kane's rage.

Ronan's cunning.

Darian's obsession.

Torin's steadiness.

And she held on.

The magic shuddered.

The bonds tightened.

The sorcerer's eyes widened.

"Interesting."

His fingers twitched and the sigils glowed brighter.

Pain ripped through her again.

But this time she was ready.

Sariah's eyes snapped open.

Her lips curled back. Teeth bared.

And she fought.

Fought with everything she had left.

She wasn't dying here.

She wasn't breaking.

And no fucking sorcerer was taking her away from them.

The sorcerer watched.

His expression was calm. Intrigued.

"Strange," he mused. "You should be dead by now."

Sariah spat blood, grinning through the pain. "Then you're not as powerful as you think."

The sorcerer laughed softly. "Oh, little lioness." He leaned closer, his eyes glinting with something unreadable. "You may have survived tonight, but I am far from finished with you."

His fingers twitched.

And darkness swallowed her whole.

16

Chapter 15

The lair pulsed with dark magic. The stench of corrupted shifters, blood, and rot filled the air.

Kane was already moving.

The first twisted creature lunged.

He ripped its throat out midair.

Another one clawed for him, he grabbed its arm, twisted —

SNAP.

The arm ripped free.

The creature screamed.

Then Kane sank his teeth into its jugular, shaking it like a fucking ragdoll.

Ronan's illusions hit next.

The corrupted shifters hesitated.

Then they turned on each other.

Tearing. Ripping. Eating.

Blood splashed the walls.

Darian whispered something dark, ancient —

The air cracked like thunder.

A black wave of energy rolled through the battlefield —

And everything it touched turned to dust.

But then the magic recoiled.

Darian screamed.

The last of the twisted creatures snarled, fangs bared, eyes glowing, and Torin walked through them. No hesitation. No mercy. His first hit sent a body flying into the far wall. The second crushed a skull in his bare hands.

He grabbed the last shifter by the throat and slammed its head into the stone floor so hard the ground split open.

Dust and debris rained down.

The entire fucking lair started shaking.

The sorcerer was waiting.

"You wolves always think strength is enough."

He raised a single hand and Kane's entire body locked up.

Magic coiled through his bones, his nerves, his veins…

His ribs cracked.

One by one.

Kane howled in agony and the sorcerer smiled.

"Pain is such a useful tool."

He clenched his fist, and Kane collapsed to his knees. His claws scraped against the stone but he couldn't move. The magic was crushing him.

Ronan lashed out next, sending illusion after illusion to distract the sorcerer, but the bastard was too strong. He cut through them like they were nothing.

Torin tried to rush forward and the sorcerer threw him back with a flick of his wrist.

Darian forced himself up, blood dripping from his mouth.

"You're playing with magic you don't understand," he growled, eyes burning black.

The sorcerer laughed.

"And you do?"

Darian's own magic turned on him.

Dark veins spread across his arms, his chest, crawling up his throat.

Darian choked.

For the first time, he looked afraid.

Sariah saw all of it.

She saw them fighting for her. Bleeding for her.

And she was done being helpless.

She felt the bonds flare to life.

Felt Kane's rage.

Felt Ronan's sharp mind working through strategies.

Felt Darian's desperation, his pain.

Felt Torin's unshakable presence — waiting for her to rise.

And she did.

Sariah forced her body to move.

The chains burned into her skin.

She didn't care.

She gritted her teeth and broke the chains.

The sorcerer snapped his head toward her.

But he was too late.

Sariah pushed off the altar, claws bared, and pounced.

She sank her claws into his chest and ripped his heart out.

The sorcerer choked, eyes wide, staring at her in disbelief.

Blood dripped down her arms, warm and thick, as Sariah breathed hard, lips curling back.

"You should've killed me faster."

She crushed his heart in her fist.

The sorcerer collapsed.

His body disintegrated into black ash.

The magic shattered.

The lair collapsed.

Kane caught her before Sariah hit the ground.

17

Chapter 16

Torin refused to let Sariah go.

Her blood soaked into his shirt, sticky and warm, but he didn't care.

Didn't care about the wreckage behind them.

Didn't care about the bodies left to rot.

Didn't care about the way Kane stalked ahead, barely containing his rage, or how Ronan kept glancing back, sharp eyes filled with something dangerously close to fear, or how Darian hadn't said a single word.

None of it mattered.

Only her.

Only Sariah, limp in his arms, barely breathing. Her skin was ice-cold; her pulse was faint.

For the first time in his life, Torin didn't know what to do.

By the time they reached The Howl, the entire pack was waiting. The wolves stared. Whispered. But no one dared to step forward. Not with Kane looking like a man ready to tear out throats.

Not with Ronan's usual smirk completely gone.

Not with Darian's hands shaking at his sides.

Not with Torin holding her like he'd kill the next person who tried to take her from him.

Kane's voice was raw, broken, shaking with something ugly.

"Get out."

No one hesitated. The room emptied, and then — it was just them. And Sariah: her too-pale skin, too-shallow breaths, and the bond still fading.

Kane dropped to his knees beside her, his fingers hovering over her throat.

"She's slipping," Ronan murmured, voice too quiet.

Darian exhaled hard. "There's only one way to stop it."

Kane's head snapped up. "No."

Darian gritted his teeth. "It's the only way. If we don't—"

"She's already bonded to us," Kane growled. "That should be enough."

But they all knew it wasn't. The bonds had weakened too much. If they didn't act now, they would lose her.

"We have to complete the bond," Darian said. "All of us."

For a long moment, no-one spoke. Torin sat down, refusing to let Sariah go. "What do we do?"

Darian inhaled and pulled a dagger from his belt

Kane went first, because of course he did. He was hers before he'd even admitted it to himself.

He took the dagger, sliced his palm open, and pressed his bleeding hand to the pulse at her throat.

"You are mine," he rasped, voice barely above a whisper. "Mine to protect. Mine to fight beside. Mine to fucking love."

His blood seeped into her skin, into the bond, and the world shook.

For a second, nothing happened. Then the bond flared, and Kane felt a weak, trembling pull. She was still there.

That was enough to make him breathe again.

"Move over, Alpha. Let a real charmer have a turn."

Ronan's voice was rough. Too light.

He took the dagger, dragged it across his palm, and pressed it against Sariah's lips.

"You were mine first," he murmured. "Remember that, little lion? You came to me before any of them."

Blood dripped onto her tongue. Ronan exhaled, voice lower now. Softer.

"You can't die. Not yet. Not before I've had my fun."

A heartbeat.

Then a spark.

The bond tightened. Strengthened. Ronan sucked in a sharp breath, gripping her too hard.

"Fuck, I can feel her."

Kane closed his eyes. "So can I."

But it wasn't enough.

Not yet.

Darian stepped forward last, hands shaking. His breath was uneven. He had done this to her. He was the one who'd put her here.

He took the dagger, but his hands trembled too much to use it.

Kane grabbed his wrist. "Do it."

Darian's throat bobbed.

Then he sliced his palm. Pressed it to her heart.

"I never wanted this bond." His voice was shaky, broken. "I fought it. I tried to sever it. I failed." He swallowed hard. "But if you die, I swear to the gods, I'll burn this city to the ground."

The bond snapped back into place.

And Sariah inhaled sharply. Her body arched as the magic exploded outward and the air crackled. Suddenly, she gasped, sucking in air like she was drowning.

The bonds.

Stronger than ever.

Tangled, unbreakable, unforgiving.

She blinked up at them.

Kane. Wild-eyed, feral, shaking.

Ronan. Smirking, but his hands were too tight on her skin.

Darian. Looking at her like she was a goddamn miracle.

Torin. Silent. Steady. The only thing keeping her anchored.

Sariah licked her lips.

"What the fuck did you do?"

18

Chapter 17

The room was quiet.

For the first time in days, there was no growling, no shouting, no bloodshed. Just her and Torin.

The others had left because she asked, not because they wanted to.

She had felt Kane's frustration, Ronan's reluctant amusement, Darian's tension.

But most of all, she had felt Torin, and the way he needed to be alone with her.

Now, he was just sitting there.

He hadn't moved from the chair beside her bed. His arms were crossed, his face unreadable, his body too still.

But his eyes told her everything.

Torin the steady one.

The calm one.

The one who stood at the edges while the others took what they wanted.

Now, looking at him, she realized she had been wrong.

He wasn't calm.

He wasn't unaffected.

He had just been waiting for her to see him,

for her to choose him. And when she finally held out her hand, offering him the one thing he never asked for, Torin's breath shook as though his entire world had just changed.

"You're not bonded to me. Not fully."

Torin didn't blink, and he didn't look away. She swallowed.

"Do you want to be?"

For a long moment, Torin didn't move.

And then he did, just enough to pull a knife from his belt. Without a word — he cut himself.

Sariah's chest tightened, but not from fear. From something much deeper.

Torin watched her, waiting.

So she reached for her own blade, and did the same. Their blood mixed, sinking into their skin, into the bond, into something ancient and unbreakable.

This time, when the bond snapped into place, it wasn't fire. It wasn't desperation. It was steady. Solid. Unshakable. Like Torin. Sariah exhaled slowly. The room felt different. The bond felt different. Warmer. Stronger. Torin's eyes had darkened but not with lust or hunger. With something deeper. Something too big for words. Sariah's chest tightened, and before she could think—before she could stop herself—She kissed him. Torin froze for half a second. His hands curled around her waist, lifting her into his lap, holding her like she was something precious, something he refused to let go of. The kiss was soft, slow, steady.

A direct contrast to everything else.

To Kane's desperation.

To Ronan's cunning games.

To Darian's raw, painful obsession.

Torin didn't take or demand, didn't force anything upon her. He just let her have him at her own pace, and when her fingers curled in his hair, when she whispered his name against his lips—That was when he let himself move.

Let himself have her.

Slow. Reverent.

Like he had all the time in the world.

Like she was the only thing that had ever mattered. His hands traced gently over her bare skin, memorizing every inch. No rush. No urgency. Just worship. Because that's what this was. She was letting him in.

He didn't waste a second of it.

Sariah had never felt so safe or so wanted, not as a conquest or a prize but as herself.

The bond hummed between them, warm and steady, an anchor that had always been waiting for her. And when he finally pushed inside her, slow, deep — Sariah felt him completely, and gods it was different. There was no rush, no desperation. Just Torin, moving inside her like he was searching for something. Like he was learning her. Like he had all the time in the world to make sure she felt it. And fuck, she did. She felt each thrust deep in her bones. A slow, aching kind of pleasure that built inside her like a storm, rolling through her body in steady, unshakable waves. She had never had tender sex before. Had never been touched like this. Like she was fragile. Like she was precious.

Sariah liked it.

She was so warm. So soft beneath him. Torin had never had this. Never had someone who trusted him like this. Never had someone let him in. Not like this. Not like her. He wanted to memorize every inch of her. Wanted to feel her come apart in his arms, to watch her break and know that he had put her back together. So he kept going. Slow. Deep. Unshakable.

Until her breathing turned ragged.

Until her nails dug into his back.

Until her body arched, her thighs tightening around him, her lips parting on a gasp—She shattered. Sariah's release ripped through her, hot and slow and all-consuming, and Torin felt it the second it happened. Felt the way she tightened around him, how she trembled in his arms, how she gasped his name.

Fuck, that was it for him. Torin let go and followed her into the abyss, his own release tearing through him, raw and deep and devastating.

His body tensed above her, his breath catching, his fingers gripping her like he would never let go. And when the pleasure finally ebbed, leaving them shaking, breathless, utterly wrecked—Torin just held her. Didn't move. Didn't pull away.

He wasn't done memorizing this. He wasn't done having her, being hers.

When she finally stirred, pressing her lips to his shoulder, her fingers tracing light patterns over his back, Torin just whispered, low and quiet and unshakable.

"You're not allowed to do that again."

Torin's voice was hoarse, his breath still unsteady. But when she lifted her head to look at him, she knew he meant it. Not just the bonding. Not just this moment. All of it. He would never survive losing her. Sariah smiled against his skin.

"Yes, Alpha."

19

Chapter 18

Sariah felt the others through the bond long before she stepped into the room.

Kane's barely-contained fury.

Ronan's uncharacteristic silence.

Darian's absence.

Now, as the room closed around her, there was something new in her blood. A feeling that hadn't been there before, something warm and right. A sense of completion. Wholeness. It was subtle, a shift deep inside her, a final piece clicking into place. This was what it meant to be fully bonded, no more loose threads left to tie. Torin's presence filled the missing space. Steady, warm, grounding. It drew her to him and pulled the others closer. What about the rest of them? Kane, Ronan? The second they saw her, she felt their relief crashing over her in a wave that nearly took her breath away.

Kane reached her in two long strides.

He didn't grab her. Didn't demand anything. Just touched. His hands found her waist, her throat, like he needed proof she was flesh and blood and not some ghost. Ronan's usual smirk was nowhere to be found. For once, he didn't have a quick word or sharp grin. He exhaled, nothing but a breath and a grazing of fingers over the inside of her wrist — a silent confirmation that meant more than all his teasing. Torin stayed where he was, massive arms crossed, but she could feel him, solid, unshaken, and unmovable as a mountain.

Darian wasn't there.

And they all knew why. Sariah felt him hovering on the edges of their awareness, her senses tuned to the tangled mess of emotions that pulsed through their bond like a raw wound. Darian had stayed away, the absence like a gaping hole in her chest that refused to close.

It was late when he finally came.

Sariah felt him first, but not the way she expected. Not through the bond. Not completely. She felt the pressure of him, the gravity of his presence, lingering just outside the door, heavy and hesitant, like he couldn't decide whether to come in or curl back into the darkness that gnawed at him.

Sariah sighed, the sound barely breaking the tense air. She felt his guilt chewing through him, the jagged edges of his thoughts cutting into her mind; felt his self-hatred like a slow poison, curling tighter and tighter until she almost couldn't breathe.

"Darian," she said, not bothering to raise her voice. "You can come in."

A long pause. Then, the door creaked open, the hesitation loud and clear in every slow inch.

He looked wrecked.. Dark circles marred the smooth skin beneath his eyes; his hands trembled at his sides, all the steadiness stripped from him. The others had never seen him like this, and resentment flared through the room like wildfire. Kane was on his feet instantly, the chair skidding backward as he stood. A feral sound tore from deep in his chest, fangs bared, muscles tight with explosive fury.

"You've got some fucking nerve—"

The words shot out like bullets, loaded with anger and the sharp edge of betrayal. But before Sariah could find her breath enough to cut in, to diffuse the threat of violence sparking all around, Darian did the last thing any of them expected.

He dropped to his knees.

Kane's rage stalled mid-breath, a sound like a snarl choked into silence. He stood there, shock freezing him where he loomed, every inch of him wound tight with the instinct to strike. This was not what he expected; not what any of them expected. His eyes narrowed, furious and uncomprehending. Ronan's brows lifted, startled. His mouth twitched, words poised and ready, but even his quick tongue stumbled in the face of Darian's unexpected submission. For once, he was speechless. Torin didn't move from his spot at the far wall, a massive, brooding shadow that watched without a word. Though he stayed rooted in place, his eyes flickered with surprise. They didn't waver. Didn't miss a thing.

Darian had his head bowed, fists clenched hard against his thighs. He looked like he was folding in on himself, collapsing under the weight of his own confession. "I betrayed you." His voice was low, hoarse, edged with something too raw to name. The truth of it hung in the air like a specter, bleeding into the silence that followed. Sariah exhaled slowly, the sound more tired than angry. "Yeah," she said, her voice carrying a mix of acknowledgment and hurt. "You did." Her words cut like a knife through the tension, echoing in the stunned quiet.

Darian swallowed, the movement visible even from where Sariah stood. "I thought I wanted to break the bond." The words were hoarse, forced, ripped from his throat like a wound torn open. His hands curled tighter, his breathing uneven. "I told myself I hated it. That it was a mistake." His fingers curled into fists, nails biting into his palms. His next breath was unsteady, weighted with despair. "But the second I felt it start to fade— " A sharp inhale.

A slight tremor in his voice.

Then, his gaze lifted.

His eyes were ruined.

Sariah watched the others carefully, the shifting tides of emotion battering her senses. She felt Kane's fury surge and swell, a red-hot pulse that threatened to explode. Felt Ronan's disbelief crackle like static, electrifying the air around him. Felt Torin's quiet, steadfast presence, unfazed but waiting, watchful. And beneath it all, she felt Darian's devastation, the full brunt of it crashing through her like a tidal wave. It was a storm of anguish, of regret, and the magnitude of it pulled her under, made breathing hard.

"I knew," Darian said, his voice breaking like fractured glass. "I fucking knew I had just made the biggest mistake of my life." The confession spilled out, raw and unfiltered, leaving him open and vulnerable in a way none of them had ever seen. The weight of his words pressed down on the room, compressing the air until it was thick enough to strangle. They all knew what it took for him to admit it. To show this kind of weakness.

The silence that followed was absolute, suffocating.

It lasted less than a heartbeat.

Kane moved in a blur of motion, fangs flashing, claws unsheathed, already lunging.

Sariah stepped in.

Pressed herself against his chest.

And Kane stopped.

His body vibrated with rage, his breath ragged, but he didn't shove her aside.

And she was the only thing keeping him from killing Darian where he knelt.

"And what do you want, Darian?" Ronan's voice was dark, sharp, almost unrecognizable.

"I want her back."

The second the words left his mouth, Kane growled, stepping forward again.

Torin finally spoke. "You think she's just going to forgive you?"

His voice was quiet. Steady. Dangerous.

Darian didn't flinch. "No." His voice cracked. "I don't deserve forgiveness."

He looked at Sariah. "But I'm asking for it anyway."

For the first time since he'd walked in, Sariah let herself feel him.

She felt his guilt, his regret, the hollow ache in his chest. Beneath it was something deeper, desperate. The bond felt different: it wasn't as strong as the others, not yet, but it was there. Faint, trembling, waiting for her.

"I should have never let you go," he whispered. "I should have fought for you." His hands dug into his thighs, his whole body tense with restraint. "I will never stop fighting for you again."

Sariah inhaled slowly as the heat of Kane's fury swelled behind her.

She stepped forward.

One step.

Two.

Until she was right in front of Darian.

Until she was close enough to touch.

Darian's breath hitched as

she tilted his chin up and, forced him to meet her eyes.

"Get up, Darian."

Chapter 19

Darian had known this was coming.

From the moment Kane let him live, from the second he was dragged back to The Howl, barely breathing, he had known. Kane wasn't done with him. Not yet.

So when he stood before them now, he wasn't surprised.

This was his price.

Kane leaned against the battered wooden table in the war room, arms folded, silver eyes locked onto Darian like a wolf sizing up the weakest member of the pack. The dim candlelight flickered against his sharp features, casting jagged shadows across the walls.

Darian didn't speak.

He didn't need to.

Kane finally broke the silence. "You want to make this right?"

Darian's jaw clenched, but he nodded once. Yes.

Kane leaned forward, still as stone, as if waiting for a crack to show. "Then you're going to kill Marcus, to prove to us that you truly are with us."

The words landed like a knife to the gut. No hesitation. No mercy.

The name sat heavy in the room. Marcus wasn't just a name. He'd taught Darian how to lie with a smile. How to kill without remorse. Killing him wouldn't be justice. It would be a reckoning.

Marcus. Second-in-command of the Rooks. A strategist, a fighter—a man who never let his guard down.

And now, Darian had to make sure he never woke up again.

Darian barely moved, barely breathed, until finally, he nodded.

Ronan let out a low whistle, lounging against the back wall with his usual lazy arrogance. His dark eyes swept between them all, alive with mischief and danger. "Shit, Kane. You couldn't have picked an easier target?" He flicked a glance at Darian, smirking like this was all a joke for his amusement. "You do realize Marcus will have half the Rooks wrapped around him like a fucking shield, yeah?"

Kane didn't even blink. "Then he'd better not get caught."

Torin, silent as ever, watched from his usual place in the corner, arms crossed over his massive chest. And Sariah stood with arms crossed, eyes fixed on Darian. The lioness stared down the snake, watching to see if he would slither away or strike.

Darian lifted his chin. He had expected this. A test. A death sentence. A way to prove himself to them. Or a way to die trying. But he would not plead. He would not crawl.

"Fine," Darian said, voice steady. "I'll handle it."

Kane's eyes remained fixed and unyielding on Darian as if his every move had already been calculated. "You leave tonight," he ordered, the finality in his voice as cold and sharp as a steel trap closing in.

Darian accepted the command with a silent nod, showing no hesitation, no fear, even as the enormity of the task settled on his shoulders like a noose. There was no reason to drag this out. No reason to delay the inevitable. He turned to leave, casting a glance at the others and for a moment, the room felt as if it was closing in on him, tightening like a coil around his throat, waiting to see if he would choke.

It was Sariah's stare that followed him as he moved toward the door, the weight of her eyes like a wound across his back. Her golden gaze flared with a heat that was more than contempt, more than curiosity. It was a challenge, burning into him, demanding an answer he wasn't sure he could give. Could he do it? Could he kill Marcus and come back alive? The unspoken question clawed at him, raw and relentless. Would he come back?

Darian set his jaw, forcing himself to meet her eyes. He wouldn't show weakness. Not to her. Not to any of them. He smirked, letting his mouth twist with a mixture of arrogance and defiance.

"Try not to miss me too much, little lion." It was the kind of taunt that used to set her off, the kind that used to spark a fire in her eyes, but now she didn't rise to the bait. Now, she only watched him, a predator toying with prey, gauging whether he had the strength to survive.

Sariah's lips curved, not quite a smile, not quite a sneer. "Don't make me regret sparing you." The words were cutting, but beneath the edge, Darian heard something else. A tremor of uncertainty, a quiver of mistrust. They rang too hollow, too brittle, as if she was trying to convince herself of something she couldn't quite believe. As if she was afraid he might not return and hated herself for caring. But he didn't let the doubt touch him. Not hers. Not his own. Darian didn't look back. The door closed behind him. The room exhaled. Sariah shouldn't care. But her fingers curled into fists. And the weight in her chest felt a hell of a lot like regret.

Sariah hadn't slept since Darian left into the night and into danger, and she sure as hell wasn't sleeping now.

She sat on the edge of her bed, staring at the window while the moonlight cut silver bars across the room: a prison she couldn't escape from. The night stretched out too long, too still. It felt like each second dragged razor claws across her skin. Darian had been gone for hours. Too many fucking hours. No word. No sign. No guarantee he was even still breathing.

It was stupid to care, she told herself. She shouldn't. She wouldn't. Caring meant weakness. Meant compromise. He was a snake. A traitor. A liar. And even if they had saved his life, even if Kane wanted him as part of this insane, fragile alliance, he was the last person she should worry about. But she did. And like a splinter, it hurt worse the deeper it lodged in her heart. Her fingers drummed restlessly against her knee, faster and faster.

Ronan, lounging on the couch across from her, watched it all with an infuriating smirk. "Careful, love. You're starting to look like you give a damn."

He put one arm behind his head, the other dangling off the couch as if he had nowhere in the world to be but here, teasing her.

Sariah shot him a glare, heat in her voice. "Shut up."

Ronan just stretched lazily, unbothered as always. "I mean, hey, if he dies, that's one less bond fucking up your head, yeah?" His tone was light, but she didn't miss the edge beneath it.

Sariah's jaw clenched. She didn't want to talk about that. Didn't want to think about the bonds at all. She wanted to pretend they didn't pull at her like the strings of a marionette. Wanted to pretend they didn't tangle her up in knots she couldn't untie.

Ronan hummed, tilting his head like a crow watching something interesting. "You're worried."

"No, I'm not."

His smirk sharpened. "Liar."

Sariah glared at him, but her heartbeat was too fucking loud.

Ronan stretched lazily, but something flickered in his dark eyes. "Tell yourself whatever you want, love. But if he doesn't come back—"

He let the words hang.

That pissed her off even more.

Chapter 20

Sariah couldn't fucking breathe.

Not from fear. From the bond.

The silence stretched. Thin. Straining. Ready to snap. Darian was out there in the dark, bleeding, killing, or worse dying. And she felt it, felt the pull of it like a whisper in the back of her skull.

It was driving her mad.

She had tried to ignore it, tried to drown it out. But no amount of pacing, no amount of forcing herself to sit still, could kill the itch under her skin.

Ronan always moved like a shadow, smooth and effortless, slipping into her space like he belonged there.

Because, really, he did.

"You're spiraling, love." His voice was low, rough velvet, sliding down her spine like a promise. He was watching her, dark eyes gleaming under the low lantern light.

She exhaled sharply. "I'm fine."

Ronan tilted his head. Smirked. "That's adorable."

He moved.

Fast.

She should've shoved him away. Should've told him to fuck off. But all that came out was a gasp. His hands braced her hips, yanking her flush against him as his mouth crashed onto hers. It was sharp. Hungry. All tongue and teeth. Sariah gasped, arched, then gave in. Because Ronan didn't just kiss.

He devoured.

His fingers tightened, gripping her with just enough force to make her shudder. His tongue slid past her lips, teasing, coaxing her deeper into the heat of it, into him.

She met him stroke for stroke, bite for bite, until her head was spinning, until the ache in her chest wasn't fear for Darian, but something hotter, rawer.

Ronan broke the kiss with a low, pleased growl, nipping at her swollen lip.

"That's better," he muttered, thumb tracing the slick curve of her mouth. "But you're still thinking too much."

A dark chuckle came from behind her.

Kane.

The air changed when he stepped closer and Sariah stiffened, it felt heavy. Possessive. Like Kane had already decided how this night was going to go.

She turned her head just in time to see his golden eyes darken.

Ronan chuckled. "Oh, he's jealous."

Kane didn't answer because in the next breath he was behind her. Pressing into her back.

Caging her in.

"Open," he ordered against her ear, his voice a growl that made her stomach clench.

She barely had time to react before his fingers gripped her jaw and turned her mouth to his.

The kiss was brutal.

All dominance, all raw heat, all fucking Kane.

His teeth dragged over her bottom lip before he sank into her, deep and claiming, his body heat melting into hers.

Her knees almost buckled.

Big, rough hands steadied her, slid over her hips.

Torin.

Oh, fuck.

A low, steady rumble came from his chest as he gripped her waist, solid and unyielding.

Not demanding. Not rushing.

Just holding her in place and keeping her grounded while Ronan and Kane lit her on fire.

Kane pulled back from the kiss, panting, watching her. His smirk was pure sin.

"You want more?"

Sariah was already wrecked, breathless, pupils blown wide, and they had barely fucking started.

But she wasn't giving him the satisfaction of begging.

Instead, she licked her lips, his taste still on her tongue, and smirked.

"Make me."

Kane fucking growled.

Then Ronan laughed, dark and pleased.

"That's my girl."

Torin moved. His hands slid up her stomach, over her ribs — slow, reverent. One settled just beneath her throat.

The other slipped between her thighs.

Sariah jerked, gasped and Kane caught her chin, forcing her gaze back to him.

"Stay with me, little lion," Kane murmured. He kissed her again.

Torin's fingers pressed down.

Ronan bit into her shoulder.

And Sariah finally fucking forgot.

Forgot the waiting.

Forgot the fear.

Forgot the ache in her chest.

Now, she was too busy drowning in them.

The world settled into silence. Not the tense, suffocating silence she had felt while waiting for Darian to return. Not the kind that curled around her ribs like a vice. This was different.

This was after.

Sariah lay on the bed, bare, sweat-slicked, spent, but wide awake.

The men were sleeping. Heavy, deep, and satisfied.

Ronan had one arm thrown over his eyes, his breathing slow and even, a lazy, satisfied smirk still lingering on his lips. Kane was half-buried in the blankets, one hand sprawled over her stomach, possessive even in sleep.

Torin was still, barely shifting, but his warmth pressed against her back, a steady, grounding weight. His presence alone was enough to keep her tethered.

And yet Sariah couldn't sleep.

Her heart had finally stopped racing, but something else lingered.

Something cold.

Something that whispered, this isn't over.

Her fingers traced absently over Kane's forearm, feeling the raised scars there. The battle-worn skin. Her mind should have been blank. Sated. Dazed. Instead, it was back out there.

In the dark.

With him.

Darian.

She turned her head just slightly, gaze flickering to the window. The sky was black, with no hint of dawn. He should have been back by now.

What if he didn't come back?

Or worse, what if he did?

She swallowed hard. The bond still existed, flickering like a dying candle. Even as Kane kissed her, some small part of her was screaming. Quiet. In the back of her skull. Like a fraying thread pulling tighter by the second.

It was slipping through her fingers, and she didn't know if she was holding on or letting go.

Maybe it was just exhaustion, or maybe it was the way the last twenty-four hours had cracked something deep inside her, but for the first time since this whole fucking mess started, she wasn't sure she'd ever see him again.

That thought made her chest feel hollow.

Sariah exhaled slowly, shifting just enough that Kane's hand flexed in his sleep like he could feel her restlessness even unconscious. She should wake them. Tell them.

But they were all so at peace.

And she wasn't.

She lay there, staring at the ceiling, waiting.

For footsteps in the hall.

For the sound of the door opening.

For proof that Darian was still alive.

And in the quiet, in the dark, surrounded by the heat of three men who had just worshiped her like she was something holy…

She had never felt more like she was waiting for a ghost.

22

Chapter 21

The sheets were still warm when she slipped out of bed.

She moved carefully, silently, sliding free from the heavy limbs draped over her.

Kane's arm flexed, half-conscious instinct telling him to pull her back. Torin shifted slightly behind her, his steady breath faltering for just a moment. Ronan let out a quiet, satisfied sigh and rolled onto his stomach, sprawling over the sheets like he had nowhere to be.

Sariah barely allowed herself a breath before untangling herself completely, making sure they didn't wake. She needed a moment to breathe.

The air outside the bedroom was thick with tension, even though nothing had happened here. Not yet.

The waiting was killing her.

She had spent the last few hours letting them drown her, smothering the worry, losing herself in heat and pleasure until there was nothing left.

Now, she was alone with it again.

She paced the length of the living room, arms wrapped tightly around herself, feeling the floorboards groan under her bare feet. The fire in the hearth had burned low, leaving only the soft glow of embers. Shadows flickered across the walls, stretching long, looming like the thoughts she couldn't escape.

Darian should have been back hours ago.

The knot in her chest tightened.

A sound.

Footsteps.

Her breath caught.

The door creaked open.

And there he was.

Darian stepped inside, moving slowly, his body weighed down with exhaustion, blood, and something else.

His dark hair was damp with sweat, sticking to his forehead in uneven strands.

His shirt was torn, soaked through with blood that wasn't his—mostly.

A bruise was already blooming along his cheekbone, shadowing the sharp angles of his face.

But it was his eyes that stopped her.

They were ruined, hollow, like he had left pieces of himself behind in the dark.

His gaze lifted, locking onto hers across the room.

Just inside the door, fingers tight on the handle, his body trembled from something deeper than exhaustion. His chest rose and fell, his breath ragged. He didn't say a word.

Sariah stared at him, taking him in, feeling the bond pulse weakly between them. Felt the pain. The guilt. The weight of what he had done. But more than that—

She felt him.

The man who had spent years keeping his distance. The man who had betrayed her. The man who had loved her so much, it had broken him.

He was done fighting it.

She could see it.

Darian took a step forward.

The rival gang had numbers.

They had weapons.

Most of all, they had power that stood in the way of Kane's pack ruling

Duskhaven.

Darian's task was to get inside. Get close. And take the first step toward bringing them down.

The only way to do that was to make them believe he was turning against Kane.

He had to earn their trust.

So, he played his role.

He went in with open hands, empty pockets, and a convincing lie. He told them exactly what they wanted to hear. He let them think they were the ones in control. And when they took the bait, he got close. Close enough to know their numbers, their leaders, their secrets. Close enough to set them up for failure. Close enough to ruin them from the inside.

He killed their second-in-command.

"He didn't see it coming." Darian's voice was flat, distant. "I had a knife in his ribs before he even realized what was happening."

Sariah's breath hitched. "You stabbed him?"

Darian exhaled hard.

"I twisted the blade until he stopped breathing."

Sariah went still. Darian wasn't a killer. He never had been. Now he had taken a life with his own hands.

"I had to make it real," he murmured, voice raw. "I had to make them believe me, and when they did, I burned their operation to the ground."

The gang didn't take betrayal lightly. They'd gone after him, hunting him through the streets and chasing him like an animal. He'd fought every way he could.

Knives. Fists. Blood on the pavement.

He took a blade to the ribs. A cut across the chest.

But he didn't stop.

Because he had to come back.

Had to prove himself.

Had to show Sariah he would do anything for her.

And now, here he was.

On his knees, at Sariah's feet, with blood on his hands and love in his heart.

Sariah listened. She didn't speak, because she knew he did this all for her. He changed for her. And he was hers, completely.

Then — he dropped to his knees.

The sound echoed in the quiet.

His hands landed on her thighs.

Shaking.

Holding on like she was the only thing keeping him together.

His head bowed, dark strands of hair falling forward, shadowing his face.

Sariah felt it all.

The weight of his love. His regret. His devotion.

He wasn't asking for forgiveness.

He wasn't begging.

He was giving up.

Giving in.

Giving himself to her.

And Sariah broke.

She reached down, fingers trembling as they cradled his face, and forced him to look at her. When she saw what lay inside his eyes, she shattered

"You are mine," she whispered.

Darian choked on his next breath.

His fingers tightened against her skin, desperate, unbelieving.

"Say it again."

Sariah leaned closer, voice unshaken, unbreakable.

"You are mine, Darian."

His entire body shuddered.

He clung to her like she was the last breath in a drowning body.

And when she kissed him he fell apart.

Darian wasn't just forgiven.

He was hers.

And he would spend the rest of his life proving it.

If anyone dared to challenge that Darian would fucking burn them down himself.

The second she kissed him, Darian held on. Not just with his hands, but with everything, as though she were his anchor, if he let go, he would lose her all over again.

Sariah felt it.

Not just in the way he deepened the kiss, or the way he crushed her against him, but through the bond. The raw, unbearable need and desperation coiling inside him, so strong it made her entire body tremble.

He laid her back.

His hands shook as he hovered over her like he didn't deserve to touch her, like he couldn't believe she was letting him.

She undid his pants.

Slid her hands up his chest.

Tore his shirt away.

When their skin finally pressed together —

Darian lost himself completely.

He wasn't gentle.

He wasn't rough.

He was just desperate.

His hands gripped her thighs, dragging her closer.

His mouth swallowed every sound she made.

His body pressed into hers like he needed to feel all of her at once.

This was about survival.

This was a man who had thought he lost her forever.

He was fucking her like he was terrified this was the last time.

They hadn't left.

Kane. Ronan. Torin.

Standing in the doorway. Watching. Waiting.

Not jealous. Not angry. Just taking in what was happening.

Because even they could feel it.

Darian wasn't taking her.

He was falling apart for her.

And Sariah?

She let him.

Because she felt it too.

Darian moved harder, faster, chasing something even he didn't understand. His breath was ragged, his body shaking, his hands gripping her like she was slipping through his fingers. He buried his face against her neck, lips moving against her skin, whispering her name repeatedly.

And when he finally broke and fell completely,

Sariah followed him into it.

For the first time since he lost her

Darian knew he had her again.

This wasn't claiming. This wasn't power.

This was desperation; raw, unfiltered, unstoppable.

Darian knew one thing.

He wouldn't let anyone take her again. Not without burning the world to ash.

23

Chapter 22

The night reeked of blood and war.

The Rooks never saw them coming.

Ronan moved first because of course he fucking did.

The bastard was a ghost in the dark, slipping past sentries, driving his daggers into throats before the bodies even hit the ground. His work was silent, surgical, lethal. One by one, he cleared the field, whittling the Rooks down before they even knew a war had begun.

But even he couldn't kill them all before the alarm was raised.

The first howl shattered the quiet.

Kane led the charge into chaos

He was a storm in motion, his wolves following him like a tidal wave, crashing into the Rooks with claws and teeth and unrelenting violence.

Torin waded in next, a fucking wrecking ball of carnage. The Rooks' front line shattered against him like brittle glass. They had numbers on their side, but they didn't have him: a man who fought like the city itself had built him from iron and pain.

Darian wasn't in the fray. Not this time.

Because he had already done his job.

He fed Kane every weakness, every hole in their defenses, every move the

Rooks thought they had planned.

And now they were fucking paying for it.

Sariah was in the fight. She had always been in the fight.

She tore through them like a goddess of war, a lioness made of blood and rage. Her claws slashed; her movements quick, brutal, precise. She wasn't just surviving.

She was fucking winning.

The trap was sprung.

The Rooks had held back a second wave. Hidden, waiting, watching.

And when Kane's wolves pushed too deep, they thought the battle was already won—

The ambush hit.

The Rooks poured in from the sides, a flood of bodies, blades, teeth.

The tide shifted. For the first time since the battle started, Kane's pack was losing ground. Kane and the guys lost sight of Sariah. It caused Kane to lose focus for a moment, and several wolves jumped him at once. Segan the Rook's alpha thought this was it. It was all about to be over. Torin got to Kane to help but Kane was already breaking free and killing the wolves that jumped him. He saw Segan but lost track of Sariah.

He roared, launching himself back into the chaos, determined to take their Alpha's head.

The Rooks' Alpha stood at the center of it all, barking orders, his pack surging forward, believing their victory was seconds away.

They were wrong.

Because Sariah fucking reached him first.

He turned just in time to see her coming.

His expression flickered, not in fear, not yet, but confusion.

Because who the fuck was she?

A lioness, alone, in the middle of a wolf pack's war.

She took his head.

One clean slash of her claws and the Rooks' Alpha fell.

Silence rippled outward.

The battle froze.

Kane turned, just in time to watch his victory get stolen from him.

Sariah stood over the corpse, chest heaving, blood dripping from her fingers.

Her golden eyes locked onto his.

That was when Kane knew she had won. The Rooks broke.

The moment their Alpha fell, the entire pack shattered.

Wolves who had been seconds from killing Kane's pack hesitated. The momentum was gone.

They didn't know what to do.

Didn't know who to follow.

Kane was still staring at the woman who had just taken what was his.

At the woman who had just changed everything.

Ronan whistled low, watching the battlefield shift, watching the Rooks crumble.

"Well, well," he murmured, grinning. "That's one way to end a war."

Torin exhaled, rolling his shoulders, relaxing now that the real fight was over.

Darian was fucking smiling.

Not smug. Not sharp.

Proud.

Because Sariah had just done what no one thought she could.

She had just ended everything.

And Kane had to accept it.

He had fought for control of Duskhaven.

Had planned for it. Had bled for it.

Had almost died for it.

Now, it was hers.

And he would either have to accept that —

Or challenge her for it.

That was a whole new battle waiting to happen.

24

Chapter 23

They take her like wolves, descending upon their prey with a hunger too deep to be civilized, too wild to be tempered. Let them. Let them break her. Let them try. She's already cracked wide open, and what's left inside isn't fragile — it's fucking fire. The cold stone beneath Sariah is unforgiving, but so are they: their hands, their mouths, their bodies a force of nature meant to consume her whole. There is no hesitation, no room for second thoughts. They have won. They have conquered. And now, they will claim.

Kane is the first, as he always is. Rough hands grip her thighs, spreading her wide, his growl vibrating through her skin as he positions himself between her legs. "Ours," he snarls, the word branding her more than any mark ever could. She meets his fire with her own, sinking her teeth into his shoulder hard enough to break skin, to taste iron. He only groans, shoving her down until her back scrapes against the stone, not to punish, not to subdue — but to worship.

Kane shifts, dragging her up, pulling her into his lap so she's spread open and exposed. She barely has time to gasp before Torin is behind her, his hands gripping her waist, his lips brushing her ear, deceptively soft.

"You'll take all of us tonight."

Not a question. A promise. His patience is a blade, his control a collar around her throat, and she shatters when he enters her, slow, deep, unrelenting.

She is shaking. Overwhelmed. Her mind is an unraveling thread as the bond pulses between them, feeding her their hunger, their obsession, a pleasure that drowns, that owns. Her thighs are already trembling, slick with sweat and something filthier. Kane answers her bite with one of his own, his teeth sinking into the curve of her neck, sharp enough to sting, deep enough to mark. She shudders, pleasure twisting with pain as the bruise blooms under his tongue. The sting only making her pulse harder. She is wrecked. Wrecked and taken. And yet, she whines for more.

Ronan watches, lazily stroking himself from across the ruined temple, golden eyes dark with something far too dangerous to be patient. "That's it, love. Let them ruin you first. I'll take what's left." A wicked grin curves his lips, his fist tightening, and her whole-body pulses in answer.

Darian is the last to move, still fully clothed, still controlled, the sharp edge of a blade waiting to sink deep. His gaze pins her down harder than any set of hands, watching, waiting until she breaks.

When she comes undone, she drags Kane and Torin with her, the three of them falling, grasping, destroying each other. The sound of it, the cries, the groans, the sharp slap of bodies meeting, is filthy in the quiet, echoing in the sacred space they've defiled.

But they are not done.

Kane and Torin pull away, panting, spent, but Sariah only beckons for more. Her body is ruined, and yet, she is insatiable. Ronan is on her in an instant, tilting her chin up, his cock pushing past her lips before she can even draw breath. He tastes like blasphemy and blood, like every dark choice she's never regretted.She lets him take her, lets him fuck her mouth, his grip tangled in her hair as he mutters a curse. "Fucking perfect."

Darian moves behind her, one hand ghosting up her spine, the other wrapping around her throat, not squeezing, just holding, just reminding her who she belongs to. "You should be spent." His voice is low, dangerous.

She grins around Ronan's cock, her tongue flicking wickedly before she pulls away with a sinful pop. "Make me."

Darian does not hesitate. The last of his restraint snaps like a tether burned through, and then they are lost, a tangle of limbs, of teeth and tongues, of bruising hands and desperate gasps. Her mind is shattering at the seams, drowning in heat, in desperation, in the way their pleasure slams into her through the bond. She gasps, arching. Her body isn't her own anymore. She is them. And they are her. There is no end, no beginning. Only this.

When the final wave crashes over them, when the air is thick with the scent of sex and sweat, Sariah collapses between them, bruised, claimed, her body aching, but smiling.

They are a panting, ruined mess.

Ronan hums as he traces a fingertip over the fresh bruise on her hip, smirking. "Gonna feel that one tomorrow, love."

Torin strokes a hand over her stomach, slow and reverent, like he's memorizing the rise and fall of her breath. "Ours," he murmurs again. "Always."

She is sated.

Together, they are destruction. They are war.

They had taken her. Broken her open. Filled her with their need.

But as their breath slowed, as their bodies sprawled around her like felled beasts—

She knew the truth.

She had taken them all.

9 789899 895060 5